DON'T
TELL MUM
I MADE A
MAMMOTH

KITA MITCHELL
ILLUSTRATED BY FAY AUSTIN

■SCHOLASTIC

Published in the UK by Scholastic, 2022
Euston House, 24 Eversholt Street, London, NW1 1DB
Scholastic Ireland, 89E Lagan Road, Dublin Industrial Estate,
Glasnevin, Dublin, D11 HP5F

Text © Kita Mitchell, 2022
Inside illustrations and cover illustration © Fay Austin, 2022

ISBN 978 0702 30356 2

A CIP catalogue record for this book is available from the British
Library.

Printed by CPI Group (UK) Ltd, Croydon, CR0 4YY
Paper made from wood grown in sustainable forests and other
controlled sources.

1 3 5 7 9 10 8 6 4 2

www.scholastic.co.uk

For all those marching to save the world

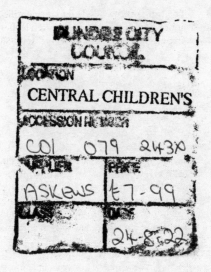

ONE

It was just a regular day in Great Potton.

A Saturday, at the start of half-term.

A bit wet for May, but other than that, completely normal.

Who would have thought that in less than twelve hours I'd be in terrible, *terrible* trouble?

Staring, in fact, into the jaws of death.

If I'd known then what I know now, I probably would have stayed out of the spare room.

As I said, it was just a regular day.

Mum was getting ready to go on a protest.

Dad was clattering about in the kitchen.

And me? I was in my room doing my homework.

OK. I was *supposed* to be in my room doing my homework, but what I was *actually* doing was lounging in bed eating biscuits and reading about the Great Potton pet thief on my phone. It was all very exciting. Two of Mrs Miggins's chickens had gone missing, as well as a prize-winning Peruvian guinea pig which had vanished without trace from the prime minister's country estate! I'd already written a list of suspects, and as soon as it stopped raining, I was going out to investigate.

As regular days go, I was enjoying it.

VERY MUCH.

Until Mum hammered on the door.

Bum. I threw my phone under my bed and stuck my nose in my maths book.

"Percy?" She marched in.

I marked my place with a finger and paused before I looked up, so she'd think I'd been engrossed. "Yes?"

Mum spends a lot of time trying to save the world, and today was no exception. She was holding a placard.

2

It wasn't *any* old placard. It was one I'd made earlier, at her request. I'd taped a big square of cardboard to a bean stick, then spent ages painting the slogan.

I'd done an excellent job, if you asked me.

Mum, however, wasn't giving the impression of a person who was pleased about an excellent job.

The opposite, in fact.

She waved my masterpiece in my face. "Save the PLANT?" she said. "The *plant*? Percy, it's supposed to say, 'Save the PLANET'."

Oh. I peered at what I'd written. Oops. She was right. "Sorry," I said, humbly. "I left out the 'E'."

"Honestly, Percy." Mum looked cross. "I asked you to do one thing. The protest starts at three. I haven't time to paint another."

"I said I was sorry," I huffed. "I don't expect anyone will notice."

Mum seemed to think they *might*. "I wish you'd take things seriously," she said. "We're about two seconds away from mass extinction. We ALL need to do our bit."

3

I practically choked in outrage. "I DO do my bit," I said. "I put the recycling out yesterday."

Mum bopped me on the head with the placard. "It's going to take a lot more than rinsing a jam jar to fix the planet, Percy."

"It wasn't *me* who wrecked it," I said. "That was you lot. I wasn't even *born* when the planet-wrecking happened."

Mum snorted. "Regardless of fault, Percy, if you want a future we need to act *now*. Why don't you come?"

"To the protest?" I peered out the window at the rain. Was she kidding?

"We're dressing as rhinos to highlight their plight." Mum looked at me hopefully. "I've got a spare papier-mâché head."

"What fun," I said. "Unfortunately, I've got a very important maths test coming up."

"Hetta Bunberg will be there." Mum carried on, trying to tempt me. "She's giving a speech on the evils of space tourism."

Hetta Bunberg.

Teenage environmentalist and genius.

Twenty million squillion Twitter followers.

Hangs out with world leaders.

Makes the rest of us look bad.

"Sorry." I shook my head, sadly. "I've got to revise."

"You won't need *this*, then." Mum bent down and scooped up my phone.

I almost fell out of bed in my effort to stop her. "You can't take that!" I made a second desperate grab. "I need it for … um … *research*."

Mum snorted again. She shoved my phone in her pocket and said she'd see me later if I ever bothered to get up, then stomped out.

I glared after her. How mean was *that*? Just because I wouldn't go to her stupid SAVE THE WORLD protest. It wasn't that I didn't *care*. It was just that I couldn't see how dressing as a rhino was going to help.

I took another biscuit and munched it mournfully. It would be nice if I was appreciated as I *was*. We couldn't all be like Hetta.

I wasn't too worried about my phone. Mum always hid it in the fruit bowl. I was just wondering if it was too soon to go and get it, when she stuck her head back in. For a joyful moment I thought she was returning it – but she wasn't.

"I just remembered that I don't think I told you," she said.

"Don't think you told me *what*?" I scowled in case she'd forgotten we'd parted on bad terms.

"About Penny coming to stay."

"Penny?" I looked at her blankly. I only knew one Penny. Penny Perkins.

She was in my class at school. I had to sit next to her in maths.

Everyone loved Penny.

According to the teachers, she lit up the room.

An absolute *delight*.

Charming.

Enchanting.

Sunny as a sunny day.

A MATTER OF OPINION, IF YOU ASK ME.

Penny thought people should be in a good mood ALL THE TIME, even if they had triple maths followed by geography and double French and had *just that minute* realized they'd left their break-time snack on the bus. "Cheer up," she said, with a little pirouette. "It could be worse."

HOW COULD IT HAVE BEEN WORSE?! THEY WERE JAFFA CAKES!

She was really annoying, and always thought her ideas were the best, even if they weren't.

I sternly met Mum's eye. "Not Penny Perkins?" I said.

Mum smiled broadly. "*Yes*, Penny Perkins!" From her expression it seemed she thought Penny coming to stay was absolutely *delightful* news. "Such a lovely girl. Her parents got the chance to go on a yoga retreat. I said we'd have her for the week."

I gurgled in horror. A WEEK? The whole of half-term? I couldn't stand Penny for double maths, let alone a *week*.

"She's bringing Chipolata." Again, Mum seemed to think this would be pleasing to me.

Again, it wasn't. Chipolata was Penny's sausage dog. Generally, I *like* dogs, but Chip was bad tempered and greedy. The other day, after school, he went for my Wotsits and almost took my hand off!

I opened my mouth to complain, but Mum got in first. "I knew you'd be pleased," she said. "It'll be nice for you to have company."

Not if the company was Penny! I collapsed back against my pillow. "When's she coming?" I asked, feebly. "I might not have mentioned it, as I didn't want to worry you, but I don't feel well. Queasy, in fact. Perhaps you should tell her not to come? I wouldn't want her to catch anything."

Mum came over and felt my forehead. "You're not hot." She pointed at my half empty packet of biscuits. "Too many of those, I expect. She'll be here in an hour."

An *hour*! Oh, woe is me.

After Mum had gone, I sat and seethed. I wouldn't be able to do *anything* with Penny around. My half-term plan of tracking down the Great Potton pet thief was ruined. *Ruined*.

I probably would have seethed for longer if there hadn't been a grinding of gears followed by a loud beeping from the street outside. It sounded like a van reversing. It'd better not be Penny already! Mum said she wasn't coming for ages! I hopped off my bed and ran to the window to see.

It wasn't Penny, but it *was* a van. A removal van. It was outside the house opposite – the one that'd been empty since Mr Farsi had moved out, complaining of rats in the basement.

Someone was moving in!

TWO

The van reversed back and forth until it was level with the kerb, then the driver's door flew open and a man with a bald patch and a puffy anorak hopped out. He jogged around to the back before rolling up the hatch and dragging out a large box. As he bent to lift it, one of the flaps flew up. The man gave a panicked squawk and slammed his hand on top.

Interesting. Maybe he had a tiny dog in there? Or a cat?

Or a guinea pig?

Oh my!

Maybe he was the pet thief?!

I peered intently through the glass. Our new neighbour looked more like a maths teacher than a villainous guinea-pig-napper, but he definitely warranted a place on my list of suspects.

Using his chin to hold the box shut, the man backed towards the gate, before pushing it open with his bum. Then he suddenly stopped and looked up.

He stared hard at our house.

I quickly ducked down. Had he seen me? I hoped not. Maybe I should continue my surveillance from the spare room? It had a clearer view of the street – and there were net curtains I could hide behind. I galloped down the hall and pulled at the door.

Weird.

The spare room was locked.

I pulled on the handle a second time in case it was just stuck, but no. It was definitely locked. That was odd. Why would Mum lock it? I mean, it was *never* locked. In my experience, people only locked doors if there was something behind them they didn't want you to see.

Perhaps Mum had bought me an Xbox as a surprise half-term gift!

I allowed myself to hope for one glorious moment, but then I remembered that Penny was coming to stay.

Mum had probably been in there to make up the bed.

It was a bit odd she'd locked the door after, but – *thinking* about it – it might be because *last* time we'd had a visitor, I'd accidentally left a spider on the pillow. It was only a plastic one from an online shop, but Aunty Sue had made a TERRIBLE fuss. She had said she might never come back.

It would be nice if *Penny* never came back.

I didn't have the spider any more, but I *did* have a rubber snake.

I checked the top of the doorframe for the key, then peered into a vase on the window ledge. Nope. Not in there. Maybe it was—

"Percy?"

Mum had come up behind me.

I swung around and tried to look nonchalant. "Yes?"

She handed me back my phone. "There's been a change of plan," she said.

My heart leapt. "Is Penny not coming?"

Sadly, it wasn't that.

"I'm not going to the protest," she said. "I've had an emergency call from work. Edinburgh Zoo. Their curly crested Chinese goose is close to death. It's the last of its kind. I'm needed for the DNA collection."

Mum works for the Great Potton Institute of Science. They store the DNA of extinct animals. One day, when they have the technology, they'll bring back all the species that humans have killed off. Sadly, dinosaurs will not be included in this big rewild, as they were wiped out by a meteor, not us.

Everyone loves a dinosaur, so I think that's a shame.

Mum walked into her bedroom and pulled a bag from the top of the wardrobe. "I know this is bad timing, with Penny coming," she said.

I followed her in. "We could cancel her if it's

inconvenient?" I tried not to sound too eager. "I don't mind."

"No, no." Mum folded a jumper. "It's fine. Dad's out later, but I'll organize a babysitter."

A babysitter? I'm twelve! I opened my mouth to tell her I didn't need one, but she started rattling off instructions, so I didn't get the chance.

"There's pizza and salad in the fridge. Make sure Penny settles in OK." She pointed along the corridor. "I've put her in the little room at the end."

I looked at her in surprise. "Not in the spare room?"

"No." Mum didn't meet my eye. She unzipped her washbag. "Could you fetch me some toothpaste?"

On the way to the bathroom, I glanced at the spare room door.

So if Penny wasn't sleeping in there, why *had* Mum locked it?

THREE

Dad and I waved Mum off from the front gate, then Dad dashed back into the kitchen, saying he had something on the stove.

I followed him to a pot of bubbling brown sludge. It smelt awful.

"That's not for tea, is it?" I asked.

Dad giggled. "Don't be silly, Percy. I'm making glue." He gave it a stir.

"Glue?" I peered closer. "Whatever for?"

"Can't tell you." Dad tapped the side of his nose. "It's a secret."

"Is it to do with your new club?"

Dad scowled at me. "It's not a *club*, Percy. We don't play *golf*. It's a *society*. The Society of Suburban Superheroes, if you're interested." He struck a dramatic pose. "Eco-activists. Climate-crusaders. Here to save the world."

I felt that sounded over-ambitious, but what did I know? "Has anyone else joined?" I asked. "Or is it still just you?"

Dad looked gloomy. "Mrs Miggins is keen."

"Mrs Miggins?" I raised my eyebrows. "*Old* Mrs Miggins from down the road? With the bunions and the pearls?"

Dad nodded.

"The two of you? That's it?"

"It'll be OK," Dad said, optimistically. "All we need is *exposure*." He pointed to the bubbling pot. "And that's what *this* is for."

I started to feel nervous. "What are you going to do?"

Dad gave me a sad look. "As you're not one of us, I'm afraid I can't tell you."

I didn't like not knowing stuff. "OK, then, I'll join," I lied.

"You will?" Dad beamed. "I knew I could count on you, Percy!" He gave me a hearty slap on the back.

"So, what's the plan?"

Dad looked around, like someone might be listening, then dropped his voice to a whisper. "You know Felicity Fischer?"

I rolled my eyes. I might have known it was something to do with Felicity Fischer.

Felicity Fischer lives in an enormous mansion just off the high street. It's got forty-two rooms and she leaves the lights on in all of them. She has a private jet and five Lamborghinis and never *ever* sorts her recycling. Even worse, her cousin's the prime minister, and when she asked, he said it would be ABSOLUTELY FINE for her to build a great big factory on the edge of Great Potton.

And not just any old factory.

A PLASTIC BAG FACTORY!

Dad had been beside himself. He wouldn't have minded if they were bags for life, but Felicity Fischer's

19

bags are awful. The bottoms drop out before you've even got to the car park. And *that*, Dad says, is why Felicity Fischer is a billionaire and our oceans are full of plastic.

Dad spends a lot of time plotting her downfall, and today was no exception.

"What about her?" I asked.

"She's persuaded her cousin to pay the factory a ministerial visit. It's this afternoon. There'll be loads of TV crews there. Mrs Miggins and I will arrive early." He gestured to the pan. "We're going to glue ourselves to the wall above the entrance!"

I stared at him. "How will that help with anything?"

Dad looked sly. "Felicity Fischer's a greenwasher! She's made up some environmental policies to make herself look good. *I*, of course, have seen straight through them. We'll be there with our banners to let them know she's a liar." He gave an excited clap. "We'll be all over the news, Percy!"

My heart sank. "Won't they just film around you?" I asked.

Dad giggled. "Oh no," he said. "They won't do that."

"Why not?"

"Because" – Dad puffed himself up – "I shall be wearing my birthday suit."

I looked at him. *Birthday* suit?

That meant *naked*, didn't it?

Nude.

Not wearing anything.

"You mean as in *no clothes on*?" I said, just to confirm.

Dad nodded. "That's right. *Completely* in the buff. Journalists go WILD for that sort of thing. I expect we'll go viral."

I let out a mew of panic.

"I know, it's great, isn't it?" Dad beamed at me. "I'm going to write slogans on my bum with a Sharpie."

I gaped at him in horror, then backed towards the door. "I just remembered I can't join your society today," I gabbled. "I've got LOADS of important stuff on this afternoon."

Dad stared at me. "What could be more important than saving the planet?" he asked.

"Nothing, Dad," I said. "*Nothing* is more important than saving the planet. But Mum invited Penny, remember? She's arriving soon. I can't leave her on her first day."

"I guess." Dad looked disappointed. "Another time, maybe?"

"Maybe." I escaped into the hallway and stomped along it. Why couldn't I have *normal* parents?

Ones who let me do what *I* wanted at weekends.

Ones who didn't want me to be like Hetta Bunberg.

Ones who kept thei— OW! I tripped over Mum's protest bag. I scowled. If I'd left *my* bag on the floor for people to fall over, I'd never have heard the end of it! I almost gave it another kick, but I didn't. I picked it up to move it.

As I did, something dropped out the side pocket.

I glanced down.

Oh my! Was that the key to the spare room?

FOUR

I gazed at the key for a moment, and then I picked it up. I checked to make sure Dad was still busy with his glue and then I went upstairs. I used the key to unlock the door to the spare room and crept inside.

I looked around. What was Mum hiding? She couldn't have started buying Christmas presents already – and I'd only just had my birthday. Nothing seemed out of the ordinary. The bed was piled with fancy cushions and on the wall above were a row of embarrassing photos of me as a baby.

I knelt down and looked under the bed. Loads of dust

and two old suitcases. Both were empty. I lifted the lid of a storage box. It was full of tusks and bones that Mum took on school visits. Nothing I hadn't seen before.

I tried the wardrobe. Dad's anoraks hung where they always hung. I checked behind them. Nope. Nothing.

Mum wouldn't have locked the door for no reason. There must be *something*. I scanned the room one last time. Something caught my eye.

One of Mum's scarves. Draped across the dressing table in a "nothing to see here" type of way.

Interesting.

I tiptoed over and lifted it off.

Oh.

I blinked at the thing underneath.

What was it?

A football?

No. It was about the *size* of a football, but footballs didn't have curly cables protruding from the top. Nor did they have a dial on the front. Or four little feet.

This was a *machine*.

I peered closer. There was a label on the back. *Property of the Great Potton Institute of Science.* Mum had brought it home from work. Was it some kind of radio? I reached out and twisted the dial. It ticked back around – but when it got to zero all it did was *ping*, like a kitchen timer. The cables had crocodile clips on the ends. Maybe they connected to something? I'd just picked one up to examine it when—

"PERCY?"

Uh-oh. I dropped the clip and spun around.

"What are you doing?" Dad looked panicked. "Mum said the door was locked. I hope you haven't touched anything." He dashed over. "That's a very important piece of equipment. Priceless, in fact."

I stared at the ball with its curly cables. It didn't *look* priceless. It looked a bit handmade. "What's it doing here?" I asked.

"A pipe burst at the lab," Dad said. "It was dripping into the room where this is kept. Mum was worried it'd get wet."

That didn't make sense. The lab was massive. There must have been *somewhere* dry to keep it.

I said as much.

Dad shook his head. "She thought it'd be safest here."

I looked around. "Our spare room?"

"Very secure."

I stared him down. "No, it's *not*."

26

"OK," Dad confessed. "It wasn't *just* about the damp. Someone's been trying to steal it. Mum thought this was the last place a thief would look. No one knows it's here. Not a soul."

"I hope she told *someone*," I said. "My friend Louis got into terrible trouble when he took the school hamster home without asking."

"That's hardly the same." Dad gave a snort. "Unlike hamsters, this is irreplaceable. Your mother would do anything to protect it."

"What even is it?" I asked.

Dad looked proud on Mum's behalf. "It's a gene blender."

"A *what*?" I stared at him.

"A gene blender." Dad gave it a pat. "Mum's spent years on it. It's for bringing back extinct animals. The ones humans have wiped out. The mammoth, the sabre-toothed cat, the dodo – *all* of them."

My mouth dropped open. I could hardly believe what I was hearing! I mean, Mum was always going on about her rewilding project, but I had NO IDEA she'd invented something to actually do it! I gazed at the machine in awe.

"Of course," Dad went on, "she can't start *yet*, not with the planet in the state it's in. The poor creatures would only die out again."

"But it works?"

"Your mum says it does."

"How?"

Dad suddenly looked nervous. "I've said too much already."

"I won't tell anyone," I said. "You can trust me." I tried hard to look trustworthy.

"Sorry, Percy." Dad edged towards the door. "We'd better go. Mum would be furious if she found out we were in here."

I darted in front of him. "You're always saying I should take an interest!"

Dad paused.

I grabbed his arm. "This is me taking an interest!"

Dad crumpled. "OK," he said. "But not a word to *anyone*."

"I absolutely *promise.*" I meant it.

Dad walked back to the dressing table. "There should be instructions somewhere." He poked around. "Ah. Here we are." He seized a small notepad from behind a jar of cotton buds. It had TOP SECRET in Mum's writing on the front.

Dad turned to the first page and read it. "Press that green button," he said. "The one on the left."

I did as he said. A tiny drawer shot out.

"You put the DNA in there," he said. "The tiniest fragment will do. A scraping of a claw, or a strand of hair."

I felt a prickle of excitement. "Then what?"

Dad picked up the cables and waved them. "You attach these to the animal's closest, non-extinct relative. So, to bring back the mammoth in a way that would mimic its ecological role in nature, you'd need something that acts similar, like an elephant."

"What about if you don't have an elephant to hand?" I asked. "Could you use something else? A hamster, for example?"

Dad checked. "You could," he said. "But you'd get a mix."

A mix? That would be amazing! A Hammoth! Or a Mampster! Imagine having one of those as a pet! The possibilities were *endless*.

Dad carried on. "Once the elephant's clipped in, you're all set. You start the timer" – he turned the dial and it started to tick – "and when it gets to zero" – he waited for the *ping* – "BINGO!" He flung out his arms. "You have your mammoth!"

"And that's it?"

Dad turned to the final page. "Pretty much. There are safety features. A reset button." He spun the machine around to show me. "If anything goes wrong, you press that twice and the animal changes back." He showed me a drawing of a confused looking elephant.

I stared at him in excitement. "Can we have a go?" I begged. "Just with something small."

"Absolutely *not*." Dad harrumphed. "Imagine if Mum found out! She'd go bananas."

I tried to persuade him she wouldn't mind, but he didn't agree. He ushered me out and locked the door behind us.

"Thanks for showing me," I said. "It was very interesting." I paused, then sniffed the air. "What's that smell?"

"My glue!" Dad made a dash for the stairs. "Remember, Percy, not a word."

"Not a word," I called after him.

Then I tiptoed back across the landing.

In his rush, Dad had left the key in the spare room door.

I pulled it out.

I'd keep it somewhere safe.

And *maybe*, when Dad had gone off to Felicity Fischer's factory, I'd pop back in for another look.

FIVE

I pretended to do my homework for a bit, but then I noticed it had stopped raining and I still had a little while before my half-term was ruined by Penny turning up. I made myself a snack and then I went outside and squeezed myself into the front hedge. I had my binoculars and a good view of the street, so if there were any pet thieves about, I had a good chance of spotting them.

Our new neighbour popped out with his recycling, so I took the opportunity to check him out again. He looked even less exciting than he had earlier and I judged him as highly unlikely to be anything interesting, like a pop star, or the head of an international pet smuggling ring. He'd taken off his anorak and was wearing a sweatshirt with a logo on it. I zoomed in.

Great Potton Institute of Science.

He worked at the same place as Mum!

Maybe she knew him?

Probably not. Loads of people worked there, all trying to save the world. She couldn't know *all* of them.

I peered down the street. A black Mini was parked outside Mrs Miggins's house. She must have a visitor. Two doors down, Mr Nowak was jet-washing his path. Nothing suspicious.

I was so engrossed in my surveillance, I forgot about Penny until I saw her trundling up the street with an enormous suitcase. My heart sank. She looked as annoying as ever, with her beaming face and massive fringe. Chip trotted perkily beside her.

I extracted myself from the hedge and waited for them.

"Hello, Percy!" Penny gave an enthusiastic wave.

"Hi," I said.

As soon as Chip heard me his head shot up. I scarcely had time to turn and run before he'd flung himself under the gate.

He travelled jolly fast for a dog with such short legs.

I charged into the house and stood on a chair.

"He thinks you're playing." Penny panted after us into the kitchen.

"Is that what you call it?" I said.

"He's just being friendly."

I glared at her from my place of refuge on a chair. I know what a friendly expression looks like and, let me tell you, Chip didn't have one.

She picked him up. "He can sense you don't like him," she said, "so he's trying extra hard."

I climbed down. "I *would* like him," I said, "if he didn't keep trying to chew my leg off."

"Just be friendly back," Penny said.

I stretched out my hand and almost lost it to Chip's tiny white teeth. "See?" I said. "He hates me."

Penny frowned. "It's very odd," she said. "He likes most people. You haven't done anything to upset him, have you?"

"No," I said. "Never."

"Unless..." Penny looked thoughtful.

"Unless *what*?" I scowled at her.

"He's very protective," she said. "He doesn't like people who don't like me. He can tell."

"It definitely can't be *that*," I lied. "I'm absolutely thrilled you've come to stay."

"Really?" Penny looked delighted. "Because to be honest, when Mum told me the plan, I was worried you might not be."

"Not at all," I lied again.

"Oh good." Penny sat back down. "Because I've been really looking forward to it!"

"Oh, me too." I glumly reached for the biscuit tin.

"Hello, Penny!" Dad came in from outside with a box of jam jars.

"Hello, Mr Plunket." Penny said. "It's so good of you to have me."

Dad beamed at her. "It's a pleasure, Penny. I'm sure Percy has some fantastic plans for you both."

"Have you, Percy?" Penny looked eager.

I looked up from selecting a biscuit. "What?"

"Got some good plans? Because I've got some, if you haven't."

I *bet* she had. Rubbish ones. "I suppose you could help me look for the missing pets?" I said, grudgingly.

"I'd love to!" Penny sounded thrilled.

"Great," I said, not meaning it. Perhaps we could use Chip as bait? We could tie him to the lamp post outside and follow whoever took him. There might be *some* risk of losing him for ever, but in my opinion, it was one worth taking.

"I hear the prime minister is very upset about his guinea pig." Dad popped his jars on the side. "And Mrs Miggins's chickens have gone too!"

"I can't imagine how sad they're feeling," Penny said. "I'd hate for something to happen to Chip."

I had a different view, but my thoughts were interrupted by the doorbell.

"Could you get that, Percy?" Dad had started to decant his glue. "This is a crucial stage."

The doorbell ringer was our new neighbour. There he was, standing on the mat. He was taller than he'd seemed from a distance, and up close his nose was long and pointy. He'd swapped his sweatshirt for a tank top, and had a papier mâché rhino head tucked under his arm.

"Good afternoon, small boy!" He beamed at me. "Is your father in?"

I was about to reply when he pushed past.

Rude!

I followed him in. The man was already across the kitchen and vigorously shaking Dad's hand. "I'm Bertie

Cray," he said. "Doctor of Science." He gave a small bow. "I've just moved in across the road."

"Dr Cray!" Dad looked thrilled. "How lovely. I'm Geoff. Geoff Plunket." He pointed at Dr Cray's rhino head. "You're going to the protest in town!"

Dr Cray nodded modestly. "I like to do my bit. I'm a keen environmentalist."

Dad almost choked with delight. "So am I!"

Penny jumped up. "Hetta Bunberg's going to be there." she said. "I *love* Hetta. I'd have gone, but I had to come here."

Dr Cray bestowed Penny with a dazzling smile. "Hetta's such an example for the young of today," he said. "You wouldn't catch *her* binge-watching Netflix."

I scowled at him. "Lots of things on Netflix are quite good, *actually*," I said.

Dr Cray ignored me and turned back to Dad. "I caught a glimpse of your partner cycling off. I know Dr Plunket from the lab. A *fine* scientist. We're not in the same department – but we often chat." He gave Dad a toothy smile. "Such a coincidence that we should end up on the same street."

"Isn't it!" Dad agreed. "She'll be sorry to have missed you. She's on a work trip."

"Ah, the curly crested Chinese goose." Dr Cray nodded sadly. "Tragic."

Dad clapped him on the back. "It's wonderful to

have a like-minded neighbour. Perhaps I could interest you in my society?"

"I'm all ears." Dr Cray peered down the hall. "Would you mind terribly if I used your lavatory?"

"Of course not," Dad said. "It's on the left, just past the stairs."

"Thanks." Dr Cray scurried off.

"What a nice man." Dad beamed after him, then turned back to us. "I have to get going soon," he said. He screwed on the lid of his final jar and gave it a satisfied pat. "The babysitter is coming at six. You'll be OK until then, won't you?"

"No need to worry about us, Mr Plunket," Penny reassured him. "We'll be fine."

"I forget how sensible you are." Dad gave her an admiring smile. "We barely need a sitter."

I stared at him in outrage. Penny was younger than me, *actually*, and I was JUST as sensible. I hadn't thought it possible, but if she was going to spend the whole week toadying, having her to stay would be worse than I'd thought.

If I could get rid of her, just for a bit, then as soon as Dad left, I could have another look at Mum's machine. I peered under the table. "Where's Chip?" I asked. "He'll need a walk soon, won't he?"

It wasn't to be. Penny pointed into the corner. "He's asleep. Chasing you around exhausted him," she said. There was a faint air of accusation in her voice, like it was my fault.

"Sorry," I said, with a faint air of sarcasm in mine.

Dr Cray was taking his time. I craned my neck and looked down the hall.

That was odd.

Why was he standing at the bottom of the stairs and staring up them?

SIX

As soon as Dr Cray saw me looking, he bounded back in. I gave him a suspicious stare, but he took no notice and started listening to Dad go on about his club. After a while, though, he said that unfortunately, he had a lot of unpacking to do and he was SO sorry but would have to hear the rest another time.

As Dad saw him out, I stared across the table at Penny. "Mum says you're staying the whole week?" I said.

"Yes." She pulled a notebook out of her pocket. "I've written a list of things we can do. Have you got an Xbox?"

I shook my head, mournfully. "I'm saving for one."

Penny crossed "Play Xbox" off the list and moved to the next item. "Where's your TV?"

I pointed to the corner of the kitchen. "Over there."

Penny looked disappointed. "It's very small."

"Dad brought it home from the tip," I said. "He doesn't buy new stuff. It's against his eco-principles."

"Oh, super." Penny clapped. "Your parents are so cool."

I gave her a cold look. It was all very well for her to say that. She probably had a telly in every room and went on holidays where a passport was required, as opposed to thermals and a chemical toilet.

"Percy?" Dad came back waving a sharpie. "I think I'll find it tricky to write the slogans on my bum using the mirror," he said. "Would you—"

"Absolutely *not*," I said. I stood up and headed for the door.

"Don't worry!" Dad called after me. "I'll ask Mrs Miggins."

"Where shall I put my case?" Penny followed me out.

I said I'd take it upstairs for her, but then wished I hadn't, as I'd forgotten how enormous it was. It took us ages to drag it into the little room. "What's in it?" I puffed, as we heaved it on to her bed.

Penny shrugged. "My stuff. Chip's stuff. General stuff. Snacks. Fancy dress. Books. I'm here a week. I like to be prepared."

I wiped my forehead with my sleeve. "I'll let you unpack," I said. "I guess it'll take a while."

"I imagine so." Penny flung open the lid and all sorts of things spilled out. "I'll see you in a bit."

I walked back along the corridor, then paused outside the spare room. I could just have a *quick* look. I pulled out the key and unlocked the door. I was about to push it open when Dad called from downstairs.

"Percy? Where are you? I'm off to Mrs Miggins's soon."

I scowled. Was I *never* to get any peace? I went back down to the kitchen.

"I'm taking your sign, so it won't be wasted." Dad was packing his jars of glue into his bag, along with

45

some sandwiches wrapped in newspaper and a banner which complained about Felicity Fischer's lack of eco-principles. My placard was sticking out the top. I noticed he'd written in the missing "E" with his sharpie and despite what Mum had said it looked absolutely FINE.

Dad gave me a hopeful look. "Are you sure you don't want to come? You could bring Penny."

"She's got to unpack," I said. "It might take her a while."

"OK." Dad picked up his bag. "Don't wait up; I'm hoping we'll get arrested."

"Good luck." I walked with him to the door. "See you tomorrow."

He gave me a wave, and I watched as he crossed the road and strolled along to Mrs Miggins's house. The black Mini was still parked outside. I squinted across at it. Was that just a shadow – or was someone inside the car? The windows were tinted so it was hard to see. Perhaps it was the pet thief, waiting for an opportunity to steal Chip. I gave a wistful sigh. I should be so lucky.

I hung around until Dad had gone inside and then I rubbed my hands in glee. The babysitter wouldn't be here for ages and Penny was still unpacking. I could finally take a proper interest in Mum's work! I turned and headed for the stairs.

Then I heard something behind me.

The soft padding of feet, followed by a growl.

I froze.

Chip had woken up and I was alone and unprotected.

I slowly turned to face him.

Maybe he just wanted to be friendly, like Penny said.

Nope. That *definitely* wasn't the case.

I legged it up the stairs as fast as I could, but he was after me like a rocket. I managed to keep him at bay with my foot for as long as it took to open the spare room door, then I flung myself through.

Chip flung himself through just as fast.

"Shhh!" I shushed, backing away. "Good boy."

"Good boy" didn't work, nor did throwing a balled-up sock. I started to panic. If he didn't stop yapping, Penny would come in. She'd see the machine and I'd have to tell her about it – and Dad had specifically said not to do that. In desperation, I pulled the lid off the box of Mum's school visit stuff and grabbed one of the bones. I held it out.

Chip snatched it, then with one last growl, retreated to a corner.

Thank goodness.

Keeping a close eye, I tiptoed over to the dressing table. The machine sat there, gleaming and bulbous. Could it really do everything Dad had said? I picked up one of the crocodile clips and snapped it. Then I pushed the green button and watched the drawer slide open.

I thought through my options. Then I glanced over at Chip, gnawing on his bone.

Mum wouldn't mind.

She'd be thrilled I was getting involved.

What could go wrong?

There was a reset button, wasn't there?

I only wanted to see if it worked. I could turn Chip into something – then after, like, a *second*, turn him back!

Mum would probably be pleased I'd tested it for her.

I rummaged through the storage box and pulled out a tusk. Mum had said it came from a walrus. Chip would make a good walrus.

I chipped a tiny bit off and dropped it into the drawer. I pushed it shut, and then I very, *very* gently stretched out the cables and attached the clips to Chip's ears.

He didn't even notice.

I reached out and turned the dial, then held my breath as it ticked round to zero.

This time, the *ping* was followed by a great white flash.

I should probably have shut my eyes.

As I stood there, blinking, I barely had time to register the sound of hooves before something small and heavy smashed into my ankles and I went flying.

SEVEN

I struggled to my feet and blinked some more. Whatever had knocked me over was thundering towards me again. I tried to sidestep, but the bed was in the way.

BAM!

OW!

I pulled myself back up and spun around.

Oh no.

Chip was no walrus.

There, in front of me, snorting and pawing the ground, was a sausage-dog-sized rhinoceros!

I had no time to think about my misidentification

of Mum's exhibit. I flung myself on to the bed as Chip charged again, cables trailing from his ears.

I sat up in horror. The cables! Mum's machine! Was it OK? I turned to look just as the door thudded open.

It was Penny. "What's going on?" she said.

At the sound of her voice, Chip swung about and galloped towards her.

"Run!" I shouted. "Save yourself!"

Penny's eyes almost popped out of her head. "Is that a *rhino*?" she asked.

"Sort of," I said.

Chip didn't knock her flying. Of course he didn't. He jumped up at her and yipped excitedly.

Penny didn't say anything for a little while; she just stared at me. "Is this *Chip*?" she asked.

I hung my head. "Yes," I said. "Sorry."

Penny swallowed. "What did you do?"

I pointed at the machine. "Mum brought it home from work," I said. "It brings back extinct animals. It's a gene blender."

"You blended Chip's *genes*?"

I nodded.

"But why? I liked him as he was!"

Chip yipped and wagged his little rhino tail. Penny sat down and put her arms around him. She looked like she was going to cry, which made me feel bad.

"I don't know why you're so upset," I said. "We can change him back."

"You *can*?" Penny said. "Why didn't you say? How?"

"There's a reset button," I said. I went over and spun the machine round. "Here, see."

"Oh, thank goodness." Penny closed her eyes in relief.

"We just need to mend the cables."

"Mend the cables?" Penny's eyes flew open again. "What do you mean, *mend the cables*?"

"Chip pulled them out when he charged me," I explained. "Don't worry, I'll push them back in. I'm sure it'll still work."

"It'd better." Penny went to unclip one from Chip's ear.

"Leave them as they are," I said. "Pass me the ends."

"These?" She held them out.

"Thanks." I pushed them firmly into the holes on the top of the machine. "You should probably put him down," I said.

Penny pushed Chip off and stood up. "What now?"

"Close your eyes." I positioned my finger over the reset button before shutting mine. "Ready?" I asked. I pressed it twice.

I waited a second or two before I opened an eye.

Chip was still a rhino.

"Can I look?" Penny said.

"Not yet." I frowned at the machine. Maybe I'd got something wrong? I grabbed the instruction notebook to check. No, it definitely said to press twice. Perhaps I hadn't pressed hard enough?

I pressed the button twice again.

Nothing.

I felt the stirrings of panic.

Penny had her eyes open now. "Why hasn't he changed back?" she asked.

"There's a hiccup," I said.

Penny looked worried. "What sort of hiccup?"

"It's not working," I said.

Penny stared at me in horror. "What are we going to do?"

I scowled. Why was *she* so worried? It was all right for *her*. Mum would go bananas when she found out I'd messed about with her invention. And then she'd be angry with Dad for telling me what it did. They'd probably get divorced and send me to live with awful Aunty Sue. I gazed miserably out the window as I imagined my unhappy future.

A movement from across the road caught my eye. Dr Cray was reversing his van into the garage.

Dr Cray!

I gave a sudden gasp.

Mum had said the machine was top secret, but Dr Cray worked in the same lab, so he'd already know about it, wouldn't he? He'd be able to fix it! It was only the cables that needed putting in properly.

I grabbed a tartan holdall from underneath the bed and held it out to Penny. "Put Chip in there," I said. Then I unhooked a rucksack from the back of the door and stuffed the machine into it.

"I have a plan," I said.

EIGHT

We sprinted out of my gate, then in through Dr Cray's. Penny puffed behind me with the holdall. "Chip's twice as heavy now," she complained. "Rhinos must be denser than dogs."

The garage was shut and Dr Cray had vanished, so I ran up the path and into the porch and hammered on the door. No one came, so I knelt down and peered through the letterbox.

The hallway was empty.

"Well, *hello*?"

I jumped a mile!

Dr Cray had come up behind us. He stood there

gazing at us, his bald patch gleaming in the afternoon sun.

He was holding a hammer.

I gulped and scrambled to my feet. "Hi," I said.

"Sorry to bother you, Dr Cray," Penny said, stepping forward. "Percy's made a bit of a mess of something. We'd like your help, if you can spare a few minutes?"

"Of *course*." Dr Cray looked friendlier now. "Sorry it took me a while to get here. I was in the workshop around the back. What can I do for you?"

Penny unzipped the holdall. Chip popped his head out with an angry yap.

Dr Cray's eyebrows shot to the top of his head. He opened and closed his mouth a few times, and looked like he was trying to speak, but nothing came out.

"Chip's my dog," Penny explained. "But Percy turned him into a rhino. It wasn't even an accident. He *meant* to do it." She gave me a reproachful look.

I felt Dr Cray needed more of an explanation. "I'm not *magic*," I said. "Mum brought a machine home from work, and I was trying it out."

A strange expression spread over Dr Cray's face. It almost looked like he was trying not to laugh. He peered at me down his long nose. "Oh dear," he said. "You're not talking about the *gene blender*, are you?"

I hung my head. "Yes."

"Well gracious, *gracious* me." Dr Cray giggled, then gave Chip a pat. "At least we know it works."

"I'm not sure it does," Penny disagreed. "Percy says it's supposed to bring back extinct animals. Chip might *look* like a rhino, but he's still himself inside."

Dr Cray smirked. "You need to use a similar species. Otherwise you get a mix." He looked at me. "Didn't you read the instructions?"

"Yes, I did, *actually*." I gave him a cold look. "I was experimenting."

Penny carried on with her complaint. "Percy said he'd change Chip back, but he couldn't. The machine's broken."

Dr Cray let out a squawk and steadied himself on the outside of the porch. "You *broke* it?"

"Not much," I said. "Hardly at all, in fact."

"We hoped you could help us fix it?" Penny said. "It's quite important. The Great Potton Pet Show is coming up, and Chip has a real chance in the elderly dachshund category. If he turns up like this" – she pointed to his horny snout – "he'll be disqualified."

"*Also*" – I elbowed Penny out the way – "this is a hugely important invention that has the potential to restore the world to a better place … and Mum will kill me if she finds out what I've done. Please help us."

Dr Cray gave my shoulder a consoling pat. "I'll see what I can do. Do you have the machine with you?" he asked. He eyed my rucksack.

I nodded. "It's in here."

Dr Cray looked strangely delighted. "Come on, then," he said. "I'll have to miss the protest in town, but this is more important. Let's get it to the workshop."

We followed him up the side of the house and down a path to a large wooden outbuilding. He pulled a key from his pocket and unlocked the door, then ushered us in. I felt a bit uneasy. The only light came from a moss-covered window, and everything smelt of damp. There was a table in the middle of the floor with a small cage on it, from which a whirring sound came.

I ran over. "You've got a hamster!" I watched as it spun its wheel. "I love hamsters. What's its name?"

"Gertie." Dr Cray turned on an overhead light. "After a dear old aunt."

"What's in there?" Penny pointed to a tank on the floor.

"Lab rats." Dr Cray said. "I'm looking after them for work."

I liked rats too. I went over to say hello. One of them was especially cute so I took him out for a cuddle.

Dr Cray pulled on a white coat. "Shall we get on?" he said. "I don't have all day."

"Sorry." I put the rat back, then stood up and handed over my rucksack. Dr Cray placed it carefully on the table before lifting out the machine with a

reverent sigh. "Gracious!" He held it up to admire. "An exceptional piece of craftmanship. I've heard all about this, of course, but I've never seen it up close. Remarkable work by your mother. Quite remarkable."

I handed him the cables. "These need to go into the holes at the top," I said.

Dr Cray examined them. "Shouldn't be hard to fix. I'll have to remove this panel. Pass me that screwdriver, Percy." He held out his hand.

I watched as he fiddled about. I hoped he knew what he was doing.

"There we go." Dr Cray stepped back. The cables were springing jauntily from where they should be. He looked at me. "Anything else broken?"

"I don't think so. I'll check." I reached over and pressed the green button. The drawer was fine. I scooped out the bit of tusk from earlier and pushed it shut. Then I twisted the dial. It ticked around and pinged exactly as it should.

"Everything's working," I said.

Penny gave a skip. "You're amazing, Dr Cray!"

"Why, thank you." Dr Cray basked in Penny's admiration.

"Can we turn Chip back now?" She unzipped the holdall. "He's asleep. Is that OK?"

"It'll make things easier." Dr Cray clapped his hands. "Come on. Let's hook him up."

Penny lifted Chip out of the bag. From the sleepy yawn he gave, and the wagging of his little rhino tail, you'd never have guessed what he had in mind.

She only popped him on the floor for a moment.

She probably shouldn't have done.

Before we knew it, his tiny hooves were clip-clopping towards the door.

We didn't panic, as it was shut.

But then he paused and backed up a little.

Penny saw what was going to happen before I did. "Get him!" she screamed.

We both made a dive, but it was too late.

The door splintered with the force of his charge.

Through a rhino-shaped hole, we watched as he galloped down the garden. I was the first to regain my poise. I jumped to my feet and raced after him. "Quick!" I shouted. "We can't let anyone see him!"

"I'm on it!" Penny sprinted after him. She launched herself into the air and rugby-tackled Chip into a flower bed. "Got him!" she yelled.

NINE

It took us ages to wrestle an enraged Chip back into the workshop. I slammed the door and pulled some crates across it in case he tried to escape again.

Penny hung on to Chip's collar and looked around. "Where's Dr Cray?" she said.

I looked too. "Did he follow us out?"

Penny peered out the window. "He's not in the garden."

"Is that his lab coat?" I picked it up from the floor. Where could he have gone? The machine was still on the table, and so was the cage with Gertie in. Maybe he'd gone to the house? I was just wondering whether to go and look, when Chip wrenched himself from Penny's grasp.

He thundered around the table, jaws snapping.

One of the rats had escaped! We watched in horror as Chip charged after it, salivating.

"Chip!" Penny tried to grab him. "NO!"

Luckily for the rat, rats are faster than rhinos. This one zigzagged across the floor and vanished under the door of an old cupboard. Chip didn't see the door as an issue – but amazingly, it held. He wrenched his horn out of it and stood there snorting, his tiny eyes blazing with fury.

It took both of us to drag him away. I found a piece of rope and attached it to his collar. Then I tied the other end to the table leg. "Let's change him back *now*," I said to Penny. "We don't need to wait. I know how to use the machine."

"I don't think we should." Penny looked nervous. "Suppose it goes wrong?"

"It *won't*," I said. "Let's just do it – then we can take the machine back to the spare room and no one will ever have to know we've touched it."

"Apart from Dr Cray," Penny muttered.

She was right. I'd forgotten he worked with Mum. I'd have to ask him not to tell her – but even if he *did*, as long as the machine was safe and in one piece, she couldn't be *that* cross, could she?

I went over to the table "You'll have to hold Chip still," I said "Or he'll—"

"Shhhh," Penny interrupted.

I scowled. "Don't shush me," I said.

"No, I heard something. Listen."

I listened, then I heard it too.

A tiny voice.

A tiny, thin, *squeaky* voice.

"Help," it cried. "Help."

I gulped. "It's coming from the cupboard," I said.

We looked at each other, then tiptoed over.

"Open it," Penny hissed.

I did as she said and peered in. "Hello?" I said. "Hello?" I squinted nervously into the darkness. "There isn't anyone there," I said.

Then something scurried into the light.

69

The rat.

It stood up on its hind legs and glared furiously at me. "About *time*," it screeched.

I almost fell over. "Dr *Cray*?"

TEN

Dr Cray had accidentally turned himself into a rat.

He was absolutely seething.

"This is all your fault," he raged, shaking his little ratty fist.

"How is it *my* fault?" I said, indignantly. I picked him up and carried him over to the table.

"You played with that lab rat

earlier," he shrieked. "You got a rat hair in the DNA drawer!"

I was about to deny ever going near the drawer, but then I remembered opening it and scooping out the tusk. "Sorry," I said. "I didn't do it on purpose."

"I still don't understand…" Penny waved towards him.

"You two went after Chip," Dr Cray explained. "I took a minute to admire your Mum's machine. I forgot I was holding the clips and twiddled with the dial. There was a flash and then … *this*." He stamped his back paw.

"We can change you back," Penny said. "It's easy, isn't it, Percy?"

"It should be," I said. "Now it's working."

Dr Cray scuttled over to the machine. "Let's get on with it then. I keep being freaked out by my whiskers. Hook me up."

I was about to attach a cable to his ear when the table gave an unexpected jolt. It seemed Chip wasn't happy about being tied to the leg.

"I'll untie him." Penny got under the table. "But hurry up. I won't be able to hold him for long."

"You heard what she said, Percy. Hurry!" Dr Cray hopped about impatiently. "If he gets free, he'll eat me."

"It would help if you kept still," I said, politely.

Suddenly there was a frantic shriek from Penny.

She hadn't been able to hold him.

Chip was heading straight for me.

Penny tried to head him off, but he wasn't having it. He neatly sidestepped her and thundered in my direction. I had no time to react before he ploughed into my ankles.

I flew into the air.

Flying into the air wouldn't have *mattered* if I hadn't still been holding the cable.

Nor would it have mattered if I'd let go of the cable as I flew.

But I didn't.

Time seemed to slow as Mum's machine looped over my head. It smashed into the floor a second after I landed.

Bits flew everywhere.

I couldn't look. I just lay there and stared at the ceiling. Eventually I said, "Is it all right?"

Penny went to see. "Not really," she said.

"Not really?!" Dr Cray shrieked. He scurried to the edge of the table and peered over. "Percy, what have you done? What have you *done*?" He pulled frantically at his ears.

I sat up. Then I turned and looked at the broken parts of Mum's machine.

What *had* I done?

I knew what I'd done.

I'd ruined the future of the planet.

That's what I'd done.

In silence, I gathered up the bits and placed them on the table.

What was Mum going to say?

Usually, when she was cross with me, it was for not doing my homework or eating the biscuits she'd bought for visitors.

This was different. I'd never ruined the future of the

planet before.

Now, there'd be no rewilding. No woolly mammoths roaming the land, back from being hunted to extinction.

Mum was trying to fix the planet's ecosystems. Now, it wasn't going to happen, and it was all my fault.

I felt awful.

Penny picked up one of the pieces and stared at it. "Do you think it can be fixed?"

"Fixed? Fixed?!" Dr Cray didn't seem to think so. He pointed to the pile of bits. "How can *that* be fixed? It's smashed to smithereens. Look at me!" He furiously extended a hairy leg. "I'm going to stay a rat for ever!"

"Sorry," I said. I really was. I couldn't remember ever feeling so sorry about something before. "What should we do?"

Dr Cray pointed at Chip, who was trying to clamber on to the table. "Get that creature away from me, for a start!" he shrieked. "I refuse to have 'eaten by a rhino' on my death certificate."

"I think rhinos are vegetarian," I tried to reassure him.

"That may be, but sausage dogs aren't," Dr Cray hissed.

"He's just being friendly." Penny hauled Chip away. "You haven't got any treats he could have, have you? It might calm him."

"I'm not a tuck shop," Dr Cray raged. Then he paused. "I'll tell you what I *do* have."

"What?" I asked.

"On that shelf." He pointed to a small brown bottle. "A herbal remedy for stress. The recipe came from my dear Aunt Gertrude. One or two drops should do it. Maybe four or five, as he's a rhino." He paused again. "Or six."

"I'll do it," I said. "You keep hold of him, Penny."

The dropper wasn't working, so I waited till Chip opened his mouth to yap and tipped a load in. He seemed to like it. He stopped trying to attack me and then went over to a corner and settled down.

"I hope you didn't give him too much." Penny looked worried.

"It's herbal," I said. "He'll be fine."

"If you say so," she replied. Then she muttered something under her breath that I didn't quite catch.

"What was that?" I asked

"I *said*, LET'S HOPE HE'S AS FINE WITH BEING A RHINO FOR EVER, SHALL WE?"

I stared at her with my mouth open. I'd never seen Penny cross before. "I already told you I was sorry about that," I said.

She glared at me. "You're always *sorry*. You were sorry the time you tied my shoelaces together and I fell in a cowpat. You were sorry the time I took a tiny nap on the school bus and you drew a big curly moustache on my face."

I hung my head. "I didn't *know* the marker was permanent," I said.

Penny hadn't finished. "You say sorry, but you don't *mean* it. Now Chip's a rhino, and Dr Cray's a rat, and they might have to stay like that *for ever*." She paused to give me another glare. "If you were ever *properly* sorry, Percy, you'd think about the CONSEQUENCES

77

of doing stupid things before doing the stupid things in the first place."

"Hear, hear." Dr Cray applauded.

They were right. I *didn't* think things through. "I AM sorry this time," I said. "Really sorry. I'll ring Mum and tell her what I've done. She might be able to fix it."

"No, no." Dr Cray hurriedly held up his paw. "Don't worry your mother. I've had a closer look and the important bits are intact. I might be able to piece it back together."

I blinked at him. "Really?"

Penny perked up. "Are you sure?"

I jumped up. "I'll go and get the instructions!"

Penny clapped. "Of course! There'll be a troubleshooting page at the back!"

"I think we're past the troubleshooting stage, dear." Dr Cray smiled at her. "I'm talking about blueprints! There must be blueprints somewhere."

"Blueprints?" I stared at him blankly.

He rolled his eyes at my ignorance. "A blueprint is

like a map," he snapped. "It shows all the parts of the machine and how they go together. Your mum must have drawn some up?"

"There was nothing in the spare room," I said.

"How about you have another look?" Dr Cray suggested. "I'd nip over myself, but you know, I'm a *rat*." He gave me an accusatory scowl.

"That wasn't *all* my fault," I argued. "You shouldn't have messed about with the dial."

Penny raised her eyebrows at me.

I didn't want to be told off again. "OK," I said. "I'll go. I'll be back in a minute."

Nothing. I checked absolutely everywhere. I'd got the notebook with the instructions in, but if Mum had blueprints, they definitely weren't in the spare room. I took one last look in the wardrobe, then ran back down the stairs and pulled open the door.

Oh!

A man stood on the step, poised to knock. I didn't recognize him. He was short and tubby and wearing a purple suit over a salmon pink waistcoat. A lanyard hung around his neck.

"Good afternoon." He peered past me. "Is your mother in?"

"We don't have an electricity meter," I said. "All our energy is generated from a home-made wind turbine and two recycled solar panels."

The man looked surprised. "I haven't come to read your meter," he said. He held up his badge. I looked at it.

Mr Amos Snook. Chief Executive Officer. Great Potton Institute of Science.

I hid Mum's notebook behind my back. "How can I help?" I asked, politely.

"I'm your mother's boss." He stared down the hallway again. "Is she here?"

I shook my head. "She's away on a work trip."

"Work trip?" Mr Snook's eyebrows shot up.

I nodded. "The curly crested Chinese goose," I said. "She left earlier."

Mr Snook frowned. "I didn't send her on a work

trip," he said.

"You didn't?" I stared at him in surprise.

"No."

I shrugged. "Well, that's what she said, so someone did."

Mr Snook's brow furrowed further. "Odd."

I didn't care if it *was* odd. "I'm in a bit of a hurry, actually," I said. "Can I give her a message?"

Mr Snook nodded. "Something's gone missing from the lab. I wanted to know if she knew where it was."

I leant casually against the door frame, like I had nothing to hide. "Have you tried calling her?" I said.

"She's not picking up."

"She's always forgetting her charger," I said. "I expect that's it. I'll ask her to ring you when she's back."

"Thanks." Mr Snook saluted and about-turned. I stared after him as he trotted up the road and got into the black Mini with the tinted windows. The one that'd been there all afternoon.

Had he been watching our house?

I gulped. He didn't think Mum had *stolen* the machine, did he?

No. No one would think that about Mum.

If I hadn't broken it, I'd have run after him and told him it was in the spare room and perfectly safe.

But I couldn't tell him that because it *wasn't*, was it?

Back at the workshop, things were calmer than when I'd left. Penny had neatly laid out the machine parts and was brushing Dr Cray's fur with a toothbrush. Chip was snoring in the corner. "Mum's boss came round," I said.

"What did he want?" Penny asked.

I pointed wordlessly at the machine.

"Never mind Amos." Dr Cray gave a dismissive sniff. "He might have style, but he's a bit of a twit. Did you find the blueprints?"

I shook my head. "I looked everywhere."

"They must be at the lab," Penny said. She turned to Dr Cray. "You work there. Where would Dr Plunket keep them?"

Dr Cray scratched his armpit. "In her office, I suppose."

Penny put down the toothbrush. "We'll have to go and get them."

I looked at Dr Cray. "Have you got a key?" I asked.

"A key?" He gave a bitter laugh. "It's facial recognition," he said. "An hour ago, I'd have had no problem getting us in. *Now*, however..." He gestured to his furry snout.

"We could climb through a window?" I said. "It's been warm. They might have left one open."

"Don't be *ridiculous*." Dr Cray stamped his paw. "It's the Institute of Science! A top-secret lab! The clue *there*, Percy, is in the words TOP SECRET. The security is second to none. Cameras all over the place. They're not going to leave a window open."

He didn't need to be rude! "What about the drains?" I said. "You could scamper through those, then undo the door for us."

Dr Cray stared at me. "Me? Down the drains?" He gave a polite retch behind a paw. "Are you serious?"

"Have you got a better idea?" I gave him a surly look.

"Why don't we just go to the lab?" Penny said. "If we see an opportunity, we'll seize it."

"An excellent plan, Penny," Dr Cray said. "By FAR the best anyone has had." He gave me a withering stare. "Let's go with it."

An excellent plan?! It didn't seem like much of a plan to *me*! Just because *Penny* came up with it! I was going to voice my opinion, but then remembered about things being my fault, so decided I probably shouldn't. I checked the time instead. "It's nearly six," I said. "Shouldn't we be at home when the babysitter arrives, so she doesn't suspect anything? We can sneak out after."

"You're right," Penny agreed. "We don't want her raising the alarm."

"Could you bring me back a snack?" Dr Cray asked. He patted his stomach. "I'm suddenly peckish."

"There's pizza in our fridge," I said.

"Oooh, I *love* pizza!" Dr Cray gave a little skip. "Bring me a big bit."

"OK." I headed for the door.

Penny started to follow.

"Wait," Dr Cray called.

"What?" We turned back.

Dr Cray pointed at the snoozing Chip. "We can't take him to the lab with us. He'd slow us down."

"We'll leave him here then," Penny said.

Dr Cray shook his head. "I don't think he'll wake, but if he *does*..." He pointed at the rhino shaped hole in the door. "Why not take him over to yours, Percy? Has your Dad got a shed?"

I nodded. "It's at the end of the garden," I said.

"Perfect." Dr Cray gave a clap.

I gazed down at Chip. He was *so* much nicer asleep. I didn't say so, though, as I'd already annoyed Penny enough for one day.

Together, we rolled him into the tartan holdall. "Do you know who the babysitter is?" Penny asked.

"It's usually Ella," I said.

"Ella? From year eleven?" Penny looked pleased. "That's good. She'll be too busy scrolling through

TikTok to notice if we're there or not." She turned to Dr Cray. "We'll collect you as soon as we can. Just to warn you, we'll be in disguise."

I blinked at her. "Will we?"

Penny nodded. "Dr Cray said there were cameras at the lab. If we end up on the news for breaking in, we don't want to be recognized. Come on."

Dr Cray called after us. "Percy?"

There was an urgent tone to his voice.

I stopped. "Yes?"

"Don't forget my snack."

ELEVEN

We carried Chip up to Dad's shed and made him a bed from a grow bag and a rug. Penny gave him a kiss goodbye, but he didn't stir.

I moved some tomato plants in front of him, just in case anyone looked in, then pulled the door shut behind us. I hoped I'd given him enough of the stress remedy. I wasn't sure when Mum was coming back, but if she was greeted by a barking rhino at the gate, she'd probably suspect someone had been in the spare room.

We let ourselves into the house and ate the pizza while we waited for Ella.

Penny looked anxious. "I hope she's not late."

Ella wasn't. She arrived on the dot of six and adjusted her hair in the hallway mirror, before dumping her laptop on the table. "I told my mum I was going to revise," she said, "but the new season of *Love Beach* drops tonight. What's the wifi code, Percy?"

I told her, and she tapped it into her phone. "The signal's best in the living room." I escorted her across the hall.

"We've got LOADS of homework to do." Penny followed us. "We'll be upstairs all evening, so don't worry if you don't see us."

"OK," Ella said. "Can you put yourselves to bed?"

I stared at her in outrage. "We're not *five*."

Penny stepped on my foot. "You won't hear a peep." She beamed at Ella. "No need to check on us." Then she grabbed my arm and shoved me towards the stairs.

We had a bit of an argument over the disguises. I agreed that wearing Dad's dungarees so we'd look like workmen was a good idea, but that wearing false beards from Penny's fancy dress collection wasn't.

Penny said I could do as I liked, but she was wearing hers.

We put the dungarees on over our regular clothes and peered at ourselves in the mirror.

We still looked eleven.

"How about some baseball caps?" Penny rummaged in her case.

"Thanks." I adjusted mine so it hid most of my face. That was better. "I think we'll get away with it."

Penny admired her facial hair. "I'm sure *I* will," she said.

"We'd better put some cushions in our beds," I said. "Just in case Mum or Dad get back before us."

We did that, then I put my binoculars and my phone in my rucksack, while Penny wrapped up Dr Cray's bit of pizza and then we snuck out past Ella and back to the workshop.

Dr Cray feigned great surprise when he saw us. "Gracious," he exclaimed. "Is that you? I almost asked you to take a look at the boiler." He peered over at me. "Did you bring my snack?"

"Yes." I handed it to him, then blinked as it vanished in a flash.

"Delicious," Dr Cray licked tomato sauce off his paw. "Shall we get going?"

There wasn't a bus that went past the lab, so I suggested we use Mum and Dad's tandem bicycle. Dr Cray said we shouldn't, as tandems looked ridiculous and we'd draw attention to ourselves, but Penny said there was no way she was walking, as it was miles.

I said I'd sit at the front and steer, but then wished I hadn't as it turned out that riding a tandem isn't

as easy as some people make it look. It was really hard to keep balanced, and it didn't help with Dr Cray popping his head out of my rucksack every two minutes and telling us to hurry up. Luckily, we were on a cycle path most of the way, or we might not have got there at all.

I hadn't been to where Mum worked before, and it wasn't what I'd imagined. I'd thought it'd be like our science lab at school, which is small and scruffy and in a Portakabin – but it wasn't. It was a huge white building with a lot of glass and enormous iron gates. A sign above the door read GREAT POTTON INSTITUTE OF SCIENCE.

I gazed at it in wonder and steered straight into a ditch.

"Sorry," I said.

We untangled ourselves and hid the tandem in a bush. Penny adjusted her beard. "Are we ready?" she said.

"Let me do a quick reconnaissance." Dr Cray scrambled on to my shoulder. I held my binoculars up so he could peer through them. "As I thought." He gave a satisfied nod. "No one's about on a Saturday."

"No one?" I relaxed.

"No one apart from the security guards," Dr Cray said.

I stopped dead. "Security guards?" I stared at him in horror. "You never said anything about *security guards*."

"Well, sorry for not pointing out the *obvious*," Dr Cray huffed. "What did you expect? This isn't the village hall, you know."

Penny didn't seem bothered. She took the binoculars and squinted through them. "It's clear at the moment," she said. "Which way?"

Dr Cray directed us through a hole in the hedge to the car park. "We'll go round the back. That's where the kitchens are. Less chance of being spotted. We'll use those wheelie-bins as cover."

We snuck across the car park and crept behind the bins.

"Wait!" Dr Cray suddenly leapt off my shoulder.

I froze. Had he seen someone?

He scuttled up on to one of the bins, then disappeared inside it.

I stared after him. "Should we hide too?" I whispered to Penny.

"It might be best," she whispered back.

We crouched down behind a recycling box. I tried to breathe quietly.

Suppose we got caught? I started to regret not wearing a beard.

"I can't hear anyone," muttered Penny.

Suddenly, Dr Cray reappeared. He peered down at us. "What are you doing?" he asked.

We stared up at him. "Are those *crumbs* in your whiskers?" I said.

"Why, yes." Dr Cray ran his paw around his snout. "Such a delicious sausage roll. I caught a wonderful whiff as we passed. It had barely been touched!"

I stared at him in horror. "You ate something from a *bin*?"

"I wouldn't normally," Dr Cray admitted. "But it smelt so good I couldn't resist."

93

"That's disgusting." Penny pulled a face.

"Well, excuse me for behaving like a rat," Dr Cray snapped. "Regardless of what you two think, it was extremely tasty." He gave a dainty belch. "Shall we get on?"

We followed as he scurried ahead, darting in and out of shadows. Eventually he stopped and waved towards a door. "The entrance to the kitchen," he announced. "The only place without cameras. No one's going to steal a quiche, are they?"

We tried the handle, but annoyingly, it hadn't been accidentally left unlocked. There was a keypad, and I offered to try and guess the code, but Dr Cray didn't think much of that idea. "You may as well ring the front doorbell and announce we've come to rob the place," he scoffed.

I pointed at a manhole cover. "In that case, I think the only way in is through that."

"I made myself clear on the matter of drains earlier," Dr Cray snapped. "So I can only assume *you're* offering."

Penny knelt down. She prized up the cover and sniffed. "It's not *that* bad, Percy," she said. "I think you'd fit."

I peered down into the darkness. Then I looked back at Penny. I looked at her and I thought about Chip, and Dr Cray, and Mum's broken machine and all the extinct animals that wouldn't be brought back if we didn't fix it. I thought about how all this was my fault.

"Absolutely not," I said. "I'll think of something else."

"Go on, then—" Dr Cray suddenly stopped and held up his paw. He looked towards the kitchen door. "I hear footsteps!" he hissed.

I stared at him. "Should we run?"

"No." Dr Cray hopped in excitement. "It'll be the cook! He's sometimes here on a Saturday to restock the fridge. As he comes out, I'll dash in."

"Then what?" Penny adjusted her beard.

"There's a button inside to open the door. Knock when he's gone, and I'll press it." Dr Cray scampered up the steps. "Now hide."

Penny and I darted round the corner. We ducked behind a pile of empty boxes.

There was a bang as the door flew back and a man in chefs' whites strode past us. He unchained his bike from a rack, then jumped on it and cycled off.

"Come on," Penny said. She dragged me up the steps. There was no sign of Dr Cray. He must have made it in!

I hammered on the door and waited.

It didn't open.

We hammered again.

And again.

"Dr Cray?" I called. "Dr Cray?"

Nothing.

I turned to Penny in panic. "Where is he?"

Penny looked worried. "Perhaps he couldn't reach the button."

"Why doesn't he answer then?" I said.

"I don't know," she said. She plonked herself down on the step. "I really don't."

TWELVE

We sat there for a while, and every now and then one of us would get up and bang on the door, but it never opened.

"Maybe that sausage roll was poisoned," I said, gloomily. "Maybe he's in there, dead on the floor."

Penny shook her head. "He seemed fine after he'd eaten it."

"There could be a cat in there. It might have cornered him."

Penny scowled at me. "You always think the worst, Percy."

I scowled back. "The worst would be that the cat had

97

eaten him," I said. "Let's hear your better explanation, why don't we?"

"He might have gone to look for the blueprints himself?"

"That wasn't the plan," I said. "He *said* he was going to press the button and open the door. And also, even if he *had* gone to look, how would he carry the blueprints in his little ratty arms?"

Penny looked gloomy. "Good point," she said.

"We need to get in there," I said. I stood up and peered at the keypad. "I'm going to see if I can guess the code."

Penny jumped up too. "You'll set the alarms off."

"If I *do*," I said, "the security guards will come and see what's going on, and one of us can dash in, like Dr Cray did."

"Oh, that will work, won't it!" Penny said.

"It *might*." I peered at the buttons.

She pushed in front of me. "You mustn't. If we get caught, we'll never get the blueprints. Then what?"

"If we don't *try*, we'll never get them either." I tried to see round her.

"*No*, Percy." Penny folded her arms and refused to budge.

I gave up. "*You* think of something then," I said. "I'm sure you *will*, being so perfect." I stomped off down the steps and around the corner and immediately fell over the boxes we'd hidden behind earlier.

I was removing my foot from one of them when it hit me.

The most wonderful idea of all.

"Penny?"

"What?" she said.

"I know how we can get in," I said.

We spent a while choosing the most suitable box. We carried it round to the front entrance, then Penny adjusted her beard and pulled her cap lower while I climbed into it. "Write 'THIS WAY UP' on the top," I hissed. "And poke some breathing holes."

"OK." Penny found a pen in my rucksack and did as I said. "Ready?" she said.

I steadied myself. "Ready."

She rang the bell, then peered through the glass. "Someone's coming," she whispered.

There was a clunk, and the door flew open. Through one of the holes I could see the suspicious face of a security guard. He was wearing a name tag that said *Greg* and there was a piece of cress stuck in his teeth. "What?" he said.

"Delivery," Penny said. "Fifty cans of baked beans for the kitchen. I'll leave it here." Then she scarpered.

The guard didn't seem pleased. He muttered a few things under his breath, then went to get a trolley. He manhandled my box on to it and pulled it, huffing and puffing, into the building.

I was in!

"Save me one of those doughnuts," Greg shouted to someone. "I'll be back in a minute."

It wasn't far to the kitchen. I knew when we'd got there because the trolley was shoved through a set of double doors and I was tipped off it. Then Greg left, taking no notice WHATSOEVER of the "THIS WAY UP" I'd instructed Penny to write on the top.

I waited till his steps had faded away, then struggled out. I scanned the gleaming surfaces and huge pots, but there was no sign of Dr Cray, so I ran over to the door at the back and pulled it open.

Penny was thrilled to see me. "That was *such* a good idea," she said. "I can't believe you thought of it!"

She was right. It HAD been a good idea. One of my best, and *definitely* better than any of hers.

"Have you found Dr Cray?" she asked.

I shook my head. "Not so far," I said.

Penny grabbed my arm. "I hear something!" she whispered. "Listen."

I listened. I heard something too. A chomping and a slurping. It was coming from one of the fridges.

I stomped over and yanked open the door. Dr Cray was balanced on the edge of a large lasagne, snout deep in sauce.

"Hey!" I bellowed.

At the sound of my voice he froze, then let out a dismayed squeak.

I hauled him out and dumped him on the counter. "What do you think you're doing?"

"I came to check no one was here," he gabbled. "I noticed Cook hadn't shut the fridge properly. I got distracted. It must be a rat thing. I'm not normally so hungry."

Penny scowled at him. "We were worried about you."

"There was no need." Dr Cray wiped béchamel from his whiskers. "No need at all. That was an absolutely *delicious* lasagne. How did you get in?"

"Never you mind," I said. "Shall we go?"

"Are you sure you wouldn't like some trifle?" Dr Cray gazed longingly at the fridge.

"No," I said. "We've wasted enough time."

Dr Cray looked sulky. "Your loss. It's this way." He scurried along the counter to a serving hatch, which had a gap underneath. He peered through it. "All clear!" he hissed.

I pushed the hatch up, and we climbed through it into the canteen. Dr Cray glanced up at the clock. "We've got twenty minutes before the security guards start their rounds," he whispered. "We'll need to keep an eye out."

We followed him between the tables into a long corridor.

"Your mum's office is the second on the left." Dr

Cray scampered ahead, then stopped outside it. "Don't put the light on; someone might see."

"I'll use the torch on my phone." Penny switched it on and pushed open the door. Then she stopped with a horrified gasp.

"What's wrong?" I peered past her.

"Someone got here first!" Penny gazed around. "It's been ransacked!"

I looked at the drawers hanging open and the papers all over the floor. "I don't think it has," I said. "Mum's worse than this at home. She never puts anything away." I turned to Dr Cray. "Where would the blueprints be?"

"There's a safe in the floor of that cupboar— Shush!" Dr Cray's whiskers quivered. He held up a paw. "My hearing is very keen as a rat." He tilted his head to one side. "Footsteps. Two pairs."

"The guards?" I stared at him.

Dr Cray darted under the desk. "Yep."

We scrambled after him.

I could hear the footsteps now too. They were getting closer.

Penny turned off her torch.

I held my breath and hoped they'd go past.

But they didn't.

Dr Cray let out a squeak as the door flew inward.

On went the light.

I peered out.

Oh no.

It was Mr Snook!

He had Greg, the security guard, with him. Did they know we were here?

It didn't seem so. Mr Snook pulled open the cupboard. I heard a jangle of keys, followed by a clunk. "There you go, mate," Greg said. "Safe's open."

There was a noise of rummaging, followed by a howl. "I *knew* it!" Mr Snook raged as he slammed the cupboard door. "She's taken the blueprints as well. Our chief scientist's done a bunk, Greg. A *bunk*."

"A *clear* case of industrial espionage." Greg sucked his teeth sorrowfully. "Life imprisonment for that, I shouldn't wonder."

Life imprisonment? I stared at Penny in horror.

"I'd never have thought it of Dr Plunket." Snook stomped furiously into the corridor. "Can't trust anyone these days."

Greg shut the door behind them.

Their footsteps faded into the distance.

I rolled out from under the desk and stared after them. Mr Snook had got it wrong. Mum hadn't *stolen* the machine. She'd taken it to keep it safe from someone who *did* want to steal it.

We couldn't give it back in bits.

Mum was going to end up in jail.

Because of *me*.

"Are you OK?" Penny crawled out too.

"No," I said. "Not really."

Dr Cray wasn't either. "What do we do?" He gave a noisy sob. "I'm going to stay a rat for ever."

"Would you like a tissue?" Penny stood up. "I saw a box on the desk."

Dr Cray nodded. "Please."

Penny passed one down. Dr Cray took it and blew his nose noisily.

"Percy?" Penny said.

"I don't need one," I said.

"It's not that. Come here."

I stood up. "What?"

Penny pointed. "Look."

I looked.

There, under the box of tissues, held down by two empty coffee cups and a half-eaten apple, were the blueprints.

THIRTEEN

There was much rejoicing. Dr Cray did a jig along the edge of the desk while I moved the cups and rolled the blueprints up. I put them safely in my rucksack.

Penny reminded us to be quiet. She opened the door and peered down the corridor. "All clear," she whispered.

Dr Cray scampered off. "Let's go this way," he called. "We're less likely to bump into Mr Snook."

We jogged after him. "Left," he ordered. "Then left again."

"Are you sure this is right?" Penny asked him. "It's taking ages."

"Absolutely." Dr Cray gave a nod. "Down here." He scurried along, then stopped. "Oh my." He flung up his paws dramatically. "Just *look* where we are!" He gestured towards a door.

"Where?" I asked.

"The DNA vault!" he cried. "Gracious, I had NO idea it was down here. *No* idea whatsoever."

"Is that so?" I gave him a suspicious look.

He turned to me. "Would you mind if we had a peek in? I've not had the chance before. The security's a bit tight in the week."

Penny peered nervously down the corridor. "Don't you think we should hurry up and get out of here?"

"Just for a minute?" Dr Cray wrung his paws and looked at me beseechingly.

"It would be quite nice to have a look," I said. "Mum's always going on about it."

"OK, then," Penny grudgingly agreed. "But, like, two minutes."

I pushed open the door.

"We need to be careful," Dr Cray said as he

scampered through. "It's climate controlled. If the temperature gets too high, an alarm goes off."

We followed him into the darkness. "Hurry!" he danced up and down. "Don't let the heat in!" I let the door swing shut, then found a switch for the light and flicked it on.

Oh my. I dropped my rucksack in shock.

"This place is MASSIVE." Penny stared in wonder.

Massive was an understatement. The room was cathedral-sized. It had aisles like a library – but instead of books, the shelves were lined with tiny tubs.

I walked over to see.

Every tub had the name of a creature on its lid, along with its picture and the date it had gone extinct.

The mammoth.

The sabre-toothed cat.

The dodo.

The broad-billed parrot.

The great auk.

The black rhinoceros.

The Sicilian wolf.

An extinct animal in every tub.

There were thousands and thousands and *thousands* of them.

I'd no idea we'd killed this many animals off. No idea *at all*. I mean, Mum must have *told* me – she probably told me a *million* times – but I couldn't have been listening.

I walked down one of the aisles.

The passenger pigeon.

The Tasmanian tiger.

The giant beaver.

The golden toad.

I walked up another.

The quagga.

The Zanzibar leopard.

The Round Island burrowing boa.

The Pinta Island tortoise.

The Xerces blue butterfly.

The shelves went on and on. Full of animals that had died out because of humans.

It made me really sad.

For the very first time, I understood what we'd done to the planet.

I saw why all this was so important to Mum.

Why she wanted me to do my bit.

Why we *all* needed to do our bit.

I stared up at the thousands of tubs and imagined a Great Potton with golden toads and Tasmanian tigers and woolly mammoths.

From now on, I was going to be behind Mum all the way.

"Move over, Hetta," I muttered.

I went to find the others.

Dr Cray wasn't feeling sad. Oh no. Dr Cray was running up and down the shelves. "It's incredible!" he squawked. "There are SO many!" He held up a tub. "The warty pig! The elephant bird!" He hopped on to a different shelf and gestured wildly. "Mammoths!" He gave his tail a flick. "Woolly rhinos!"

"Careful!" Penny shrieked. Her warning came too late. A whole stack of tubs tumbled to the floor.

"Oops." Dr Cray jumped down. "How careless

of me. Don't worry, none are broken. Most of them landed on your rucksack. No harm done." He started to gather them up.

I went over to help. A few of the lids had come off, so I screwed them back on.

"Thank you." Dr Cray reached out his paws. "I'll take those. Make sure they're put back in the right place." He gave a little giggle.

"We should go," I said.

"Yes," Penny said. "It's getting late."

"I'll just finish tidying these." Dr Cray picked up the tub of Mammoth DNA. "You two pop your heads out and check for guards."

"OK," I said.

We headed for the door. I was just about to push it open when Penny caught my arm. "Listen," she whispered.

I listened, then gulped.

Footsteps. Coming along the corridor.

I dashed back into the vault and scrambled under a bench.

"I *knew* we should have gone straight home." Penny squeezed in next to me, then stuck her head back out. "Dr Cray!" she hissed. "Dr *Cray*."

Dr Cray was buckling up my rucksack and didn't hear.

Penny raised her voice. "DR CRA—"

Too late. The door to the vault flew open with a crash.

Dr Cray heard *that*. He went rigid.

A lone tub rolled slowly across the floor.

The footsteps came into the room.

I peered out. "It's Snook," I whispered.

There was a silence as he and Dr Cray stared at each other. Then Mr Snook pulled out his radio. "Greg? *Greg*?" he bellowed into it. "There's a rat in the DNA vault! Yes, a R. A. T. *RAT*. Get here *now*!"

Dr Cray regained the use of his limbs. He legged it. Mr Snook thundered after him. Up and down the aisles they went. Dr Cray was pretty nippy and kept up a good lead, but there was nowhere for him to escape to. Luckily, Greg arrived swiftly, and Dr Cray took advantage. He shot out through the open door and down the corridor. Mr Snook and Greg hurtled after him.

We climbed out from under the bench. Penny looked pale. "They won't catch him, will they?" she said.

"I shouldn't think so," I said. "He seems quite fast, and the others aren't."

We quietly gathered up the tubs that were still on the floor and put them back on the shelves. "Come on," I said. I picked up my rucksack. "We'll wait for him by the tandem."

We let ourselves out of the kitchen and ran across the darkening car park. Dr Cray was already there, eating an old pasty. "You took your time," he complained. "Thought they'd got you. I was limbering up to come back in."

I eyed the crumbs down his front. "Looks like it," I said.

Dr Cray brushed them off. "You've still got the blueprints?"

I held up my rucksack.

"Excellent." Dr Cray shoved in the last mouthful. "Let's go."

FOURTEEN

Dr Cray was keen to start work on the machine right away. Penny took off her beard and I took off my rucksack and pulled out the blueprints. I unrolled them on the table, then put my bag down on the floor.

There was a strange *clunk*.

Odd.

I peered inside.

Eh?

Rolling around at the bottom was a whole load of tubs from the lab! I stared at them, then took one out and held it up. "Dr Cray?"

Dr Cray peered over the edge of the table.

"Gracious!" he exclaimed. He covered his mouth with his paws. "You didn't *take* those, did you, Percy?"

"No!" I said. "They were just *in* here. I don't know how."

Penny came to see. She looked at Dr Cray. "Do you think they fell in when you knocked them off the shelf?"

"I think you must be right, Penny," Dr Cray agreed. "How unfortunate. No matter. I'll return them anonymously on Monday. It won't be a problem."

That was good. I wouldn't want Mum to be blamed for stealing DNA, as well as everything else!

Dr Cray scampered back to the blueprints. "Are we ready?" He flexed his paws. "Percy, you're in charge of the screwdrivers. They're in that box over there. Penny? Can you fetch the superglue? There's some in that drawer."

"Shall we get Chip?" Penny asked.

"Not until we absolutely have to." Dr Cray gave her a toothy smile. "We don't want any more catastrophes, do we?"

Penny looked cross and muttered something about *none of this being Chip's fault*, but she went and got the glue and then we made a start.

It took a while. Penny glued her hands together more than once and Dr Cray kept getting rolled up in the blueprints. In the end we stuck them down with Blu-Tack, which left him free to bossily shout orders. He was *extremely* picky. The circuit boards had to be placed in exactly the right order and when there was a screw left over it was a VERY BIG DEAL and we had to start all over again. Then, even though I had *double checked* there was nothing in the DNA drawer, he made me wash it out about ten times before I was allowed to reattach it.

At last, we were finished. Mum's machine sat in the middle of the table, almost as good as new.

"Can we get Chip now?" Penny hopped impatiently.

"Do me first." Dr Cray picked up the cables. He attached the clips to his ears, then looked at me expectantly. "Go on, then." he said. "Press the reset button."

"Do you want your lab coat?" I held it up.

Dr Cray blinked at me. "Why?"

I discreetly pointed. "That."

Dr Cray looked down at himself, then back at me with a puzzled look. "What?" he said.

"You're … um … *naked*," I said.

Penny sniggered.

"Oh, so I am." Dr Cray's ears went pink. "I'm so used to my fur, I'd completely forgotten. Thank you, Percy."

I handed him his coat and waited as he burrowed under it.

"Ready?" I asked.

"I am." Dr Cray nodded.

I reminded Penny to shut her eyes, then I covered mine and counted backwards from three.

There was a fizz and a crackle and a smell of burnt pelt.

Penny gave a cheer.

I took my hands away from my eyes.

Dr Cray was back! There he was in front of me, doing a little twirl. "Oh happy, *happy* day!" he chortled.

I don't think I'd ever been so pleased about anything

in my ENTIRE life! The machine was fixed! It worked! We only needed to turn Chip back, and Mum would never know. She'd come home from her trip and I'd tell her about Mr Snook and she'd go and explain that it was all a misunderstanding and EVERYTHING WOULD BE FINE!

I felt giddy with relief.

"It's so nice to be myself again." Dr Cray admired his furless skin. "I no longer have an insatiable desire for baked goods."

Penny grabbed my arm. "Come on. It's Chip's turn. Let's go and get him."

We headed for the door.

"No rush." Dr Cray called after us. "I'll just be here, tidying stuff up."

I turned and gave him a wave.

He gave me a little wave back. "Bye, Percy," he said.

Chip was still snoring amidst the tomatoes.

We rolled him into the holdall and carried it back down the path. Just as we got to the gate, a black Mini pulled up outside. "It's Mr Snook," I hissed. "Look nonchalant."

"It's hard when you're carrying a rhino," Penny hissed back.

Mr Snook wound down his window and stuck out his head. "Heard from your mother yet?" he asked.

"Yes," I lied. "She just called. She said not to worry, she'll explain everything when she's back."

"Is that so?" Mr Snook gave a disbelieving snort. He watched as we crossed the road and turned into Dr Cray's gate. He could sit there all night for all I cared. Tomorrow, Mum's machine would be back where it should be. I'd invite him in to see it, and he'd feel really stupid. HA.

We carried Chip up to the workshop.

The light was still on, but the place seemed empty.

"Dr Cray?" I called. I expected him to pop up from somewhere, but he didn't.

I looked around. "Hello?" I said.

There was no reply. "He'd better not have turned himself into a rat again," I huffed.

Penny said he wouldn't be that stupid, but I checked the cupboard in case. He wasn't in there, either as himself, or anything else.

I backed out, puzzled, and it was *then* that Penny asked where Mum's machine had gone.

I looked at the table, which is where the machine had been ten minutes ago.

It wasn't there now.

Nor was the cage with Gertie in.

And the tank of rats wasn't on the floor, either.

I didn't understand. I peered under the table, then gulped. Where was my rucksack with the DNA in? I tried to quell my rising panic. "I expect he's gone back to the house," I said.

"Why would he do that?" Penny asked.

"I don't know," I said. "I'll go and see. You stay with Chip."

I ran back down the path and tried the back door. It was locked. I banged on it. "Dr Cray?" I called. "DR CRAY!"

No one called back.

There wasn't a sound.

I peered in through the kitchen window. There weren't any lights on. In fact, there was nothing at all to suggest someone had recently moved in. No kettle. No cups on the side. No boxes waiting to be unpacked.

I started to feel a bit sick.

I walked around to the front of the house. The rooms there were empty too.

Where was Dr Cray?

More importantly, where was Mum's machine?

I opened the door to the garage.

Oh no.

FIFTEEN

"Did you find him?" Penny looked up from the floor, where she was sitting next to Chip, who was still slumbering away.

"The van's gone," I said.

"Gone?" Penny stared at me.

I still couldn't think the worst. "Maybe he decided to take everything back to the lab?" I said. "So Mum wouldn't be in trouble."

Penny frowned. "Without turning Chip back into a sausage dog? Or *telling* us?"

"There must be *some* explanation," I said. "I just don't know what it is."

"Can you ring him?" Penny asked.

"I don't have his number," I said. "And even if I *did*" – I plonked myself down next to her and Chip – "my phone was in the rucksack."

"Really?" Penny stared at me.

I nodded.

"That's good." She reached in her pocket.

"Good?" I stared at her owlishly. "In what way?"

"I can track it on Snap Maps." She pulled out her phone, then tapped the screen a couple of times. She held it out. "See!"

I grabbed her phone and stared at it closely. Oh my, Penny was a genius! There was my Bitmoji! It was travelling along the high street. It wasn't heading for the Great Potton Institute of Science, though. It was moving in the opposite direction. "Where's he going?" I asked.

Penny shook her head. "I don't know," she said. "But I'm starting to wonder why we trusted him."

She'd said it.

She'd said the words I hadn't wanted to admit were in my head.

What did we *really* know about Dr Cray?

I remembered him standing and staring up the stairs at my house earlier. Had he known the machine was there all along? *No*. There *had* to be an explanation. He wouldn't have stolen it! He was a scientist! He had a papier mâché rhino head! He was going to the protest! He wanted to save the planet, the same as Mum.

I'd seen him putting his recycling out.

Hadn't I?

"Can I borrow that?" I grabbed Penny's phone to use as a torch and hurtled down the garden to the wheelie-bin. I lifted the lid and peered inside.

My heart sank.

Dr Cray was no environmentalist.

He wasn't trying to save the planet.

He was a liar.

I trudged back up the path to Penny.

"Where did you go?" she asked.

"The bin," I said. "Dr Cray's not who he says he is. He's got crisp packets mixed in with his cardboard!

There's an unrinsed jam jar! Even *I* rinse jam jars!" I sat down with a bump. "What else has he lied about?"

Penny shook her head. "He was so sweet as a rat," she mourned. "Now I feel like we didn't know him at all."

"I don't think we did," I said, gloomily.

"He must be *something* to do with the lab," Penny said. "Or he wouldn't have known where everything was." She took her phone back. "Let's see." She typed *Great Potton Institute of Science* into the search bar, then clicked through to the staff list. She scrolled through the photos. There was Mr Snook, and Mum, and loads of other people who looked super clever. She kept scrolling. Past the cook we'd seen earlier, and Greg the security guard.

There he was!

Bertie Cray.

Beaming into the lens.

"So he *does* work there," I said.

Penny peered closer. "Yes. But he's lying about being

a Doctor of Science. He works in the CANTEEN!" She jumped to her feet and pulled me to mine. "Come on! We need to catch up with him!"

SIXTEEN

I clipped the holdall with Chip in on to the rack at the back of the tandem. "I'll steer. You watch where Cray's going and shout directions."

Penny jumped on, and we wobbled down the path. "It's quite dark," she said. "Can you see? Where are the lights?"

"Hang on." I switched them on and we swung out on to the pavement. I was glad to see Mr Snook's car had gone.

"Head for the high street," Penny ordered.

"I'll cut through the park," I said. I bumped down the kerb and swerved in through the gates. We almost ran over a duck by the pond – and also a jogger – but I quickly regained control by going over a lovely smooth bit Penny said was the bowling green. "Watch out for the adventure fort!" she shrieked.

"I'm nowhere near it," I snapped. I missed the fort by an inch and veered out of the back gate.

"He's heading out of town," Penny said. "Follow the cycle path."

I did as she said till we came to a fork. "Where now?" I asked.

Penny studied her phone. "He's stopped at Felicity Fischer's factory! Turn left."

I didn't know why Cray would be at Felicity Fischer's factory, but it didn't matter. What mattered was, it wasn't far. My legs were *killing* me.

"Do you think your dad and Mrs Miggins are still there?" Penny asked as we pedalled up the hill.

"It depends how strong the glue was," I puffed.

The factory loomed ahead of us, a great steel dome lit up with a billion floodlights. I couldn't see anyone stuck to it, which was good, as we didn't have time to answer questions about what we were doing there. We cycled through the gates and up the drive and hid the tandem behind a skip.

Chip gave a dainty snore as Penny unclipped the holdall. She slung him over her shoulder and set off across the car park. I was about to follow when something in the skip caught my eye.

My placard!

Hey! I stared in outrage. I couldn't believe Dad had chucked it away! It wasn't *that* bad!

I jumped up to get it out. And it was then I noticed something else in the skip too.

Dad's bag!

I gulped. Why would that be there? Where was he?

Maybe he and Mrs Miggins had been arrested, like he'd hoped.

I pulled the bag out and peered inside. His clothes were there, neatly folded. Wherever he was, he wasn't wearing much. The pots of glue were there too, and so were his sandwiches, wrapped in a page from the *Great Potton Gazette*. Its headline caught my eye:

PRIME MINISTER'S GUINEA PIG HORROR!

There'd been a ransom demand! The pet thief was an extortionist!

I had no time to think about that now. I put the bag down and followed Penny. She'd stopped and was holding her phone in the air. "I've lost the signal," she said. "He must have gone inside."

"Are you sure he's still here?" I asked.

"Yes." She pointed.

Parked on the other side of Felicity Fischer's Lamborghini was Cray's van.

"I already looked in the back," she said. "It's empty. If he's got the machine, he's taken it with him."

I turned and ran towards a fire door which was propped open with a bucket. "Come on, then," I said. "We can't be far behind."

I charged inside and blinked in the bright overhead lights. The room was *enormous*. Production was in full swing. Huge machines whirred and hissed, and at the end of a conveyor belt, thousands of bags were being folded into boxes by giant robotic arms.

It smelt horribly of burnt plastic.

Penny jogged up behind me. "There he is!" she cried.

Cray was ahead of us, pushing a trolley piled with boxes. On top of them was Gertie's cage, and next to that was my rucksack! As we watched, he vanished though a set of double doors.

"Let's see what he's up to!" Penny set off.

"Wait!" I said. I grabbed another trolley and pulled an empty box on to it. "You and Chip get in here," I said. "I'll push. We'll be less obvious."

"OK," Penny clambered in and shut the lid. Then she popped her head back out. "I've got my beard in my pocket," she said. "Do you want it?"

"Thanks, but no," I said. "Ready?"

"All set." Penny vanished back inside.

I took a deep breath and started to push.

SEVENTEEN

The corridor was long and straight and Cray was way ahead. I sped up.

Where was he going?

He took a sudden left through a doorway. "Good evening, Felicity," I heard him say.

There was an exclamation of surprise from within, followed by the sound of a chair being pushed back. "Bertie! What are you doing here?" There was a tip-tapping of heels, followed by the sound of air kisses. "How *delicious* to see you."

Penny popped her head out. "Is that Felicity Fischer?"

"I guess so." I steadied the box so she could climb out. "He must know her."

We left Chip asleep on the trolley and crept as near as we dared. I peered around the door frame. I'd seen Felicity Fischer in pictures loads of times, and she looked just the same in real life. Her hair was elaborately curled and piled high on her head, and she was wearing a bright red suit which made her shoulders look pointy. Even though she was tall, she was dwarfed by her enormous desk, which had a chandelier hanging above it.

Despite what she'd said, she didn't look *particularly* happy to see Cray.

He'd made himself comfortable in a plush-looking seat and had his feet up on a pouffe. "It's been a while, cousin," he said.

My mouth dropped open. Cousin? Cray was Felicity Fischer's *cousin?* He hadn't mentioned that!

"Making money takes a lot of time, Bertie." Felicity Fischer shook her head mournfully. "Much as it pains me, family comes second."

"You keep in touch with my brother." Cray looked sulky.

"Well, of *course*." Felicity Fischer tittered. "He's the prime minister. Naturally I have time for *him*. How else would I get my plans approved?"

My mouth dropped open. Cray's brother was *the prime minister*? He hadn't mentioned that, either.

"Did you want something?" Felicity Fischer went on. "I'm busy."

Cray sat forward. "I've a proposal for you," he said, excitedly. "A really good one."

Felicity Fischer sighed. "Bertie, if your money-making schemes ended well, you'd be rich, wouldn't you? Like *me*?" She waggled her hand so the light caught her enormous rings. "Just saying."

"Make the most of it." Cray leant back in his chair. "Plastic will be banned soon. That Hetta girl has turned everyone against it." He gave a giggle. "No one will want your bags. Give it a year, your factory will be shut. You'll be skint."

"It'll be a long time before *I'm* skint, Bertie," Felicity

Fischer snapped.

Cray shrugged. "If you don't want to hear my idea, I'll be off." He stood up and took hold of his trolley.

"Wait." Felicity Fischer held up her bejewelled hand.

Cray paused. "What?"

"You've made the journey. You may as well show me what you brought."

"I knew you wouldn't be able to resist." Cray looked smug, then strolled over to his trolley and opened a box. A chicken stuck its head out with a squawk. "Wrong one, sorry." Cray gave a nervous giggle. He opened a second box. "This is it." He reached inside and lifted out Mum's machine.

He held it up triumphantly.

Felicity Fischer scowled at it. "What on earth is that?"

Cray walked over and placed it on the desk. "I'm about to tell you."

Felicity Fischer looked at her glittery watch. "Hurry, then. I'm busy. I'll give you two minutes."

"That's plenty." Cray gave her a small bow, then

began. "In the right hands, this machine" – he gestured extravagantly towards it – "will make you more money than you could ever imagine."

Felicity Fischer raised an eyebrow. "I already have a *lot*," she said, "but I suppose you can never have too much." She peered closer. "What is it, and where did you get it from?"

"If you stop interrupting, I'll come to that," Cray huffed. "Anyway. After you *fired* me" – he paused to give his cousin an especially nasty scowl – "I had to find alternative employment. I noticed they were advertising for staff at the Great Potton Institute of Science—"

"The place full of nerdy do-gooders?"

"That's right." Cray nodded. "I applied, and they offered me a position."

Felicity Fischer looked surprised. "As a scientist?"

"In the canteen," Cray confessed.

Felicity Fischer yawned.

"I haven't got to the good bit yet." Cray glared at her. "There was a reason I wanted to work there."

Felicity Fischer gave a snort. "What was that?"

"Secrets." Cray looked triumphant.

"Secrets?" Felicity Fischer blinked at him.

"Yes. *Secrets*. I was perfectly placed to acquire them." Cray preened. "No one takes any notice of canteen staff. I may as well have been invisible! All those scientists chatting amongst themselves! If they mentioned anything interesting, I'd zoom over to wipe their table."

"Industrial espionage! Gracious!" Felicity Fischer looked impressed. "I must say, Bertie, you've gone up in my estimation! You never even used to cheat at cards."

"I was fed up with being skint." Cray looked mournful. "Criminality seemed the only way."

Felicity Fischer admired her expensive rings. "There is something to be said for being corrupt," she agreed. "What were you planning to do with the secrets? Sell them for vast quantities of cash?"

"Exactly that!" Cray nodded vigorously. "And on only my second day, I overheard talk of something quite remarkable!"

Felicity Fischer looked interested. "Tell me," she said.

"A machine." Cray dropped his voice to a whisper. "One that would bring animals back from extinction! They'd built it to rewild the planet!"

Felicity Fischer tutted. "I've heard of rewilding. Absolutely *ridiculous*. Why would anyone want to do that? We've got plenty of animals. What do we need more for?"

"I wondered that at first," Cray admitted. "But then I began to think of the machine's possibilities! I decided to try it out. I knew it wouldn't be easy to steal – it was very well guarded. When I almost got caught, I realized I needed to up my game."

Felicity Fischer raised an eyebrow. "Do go on."

Cray giggled. "I drilled a hole in a water pipe above the room the machine was kept in. Then I alerted the head scientist to the leak. Poor Dr Plunket. She couldn't let the machine get wet, but after the attempted theft, she was worried about where to move it to." He puffed himself up. "I suggested she take it home. She thought it was a great idea. Told me not to tell a soul."

"He hoodwinked Mum!" I muttered angrily.

"I filled her neighbour's basement with rats." Cray carried on. "He moved out quick sharp. Then I hired myself a van, and pretended to move in. All I had to do was get rid of Dr Plunket."

"Ger rid of her?" Felicity Fischer's eyes popped. "How did you manage that?"

"I gave her a call and pretended to be her boss. Sent her off on a work emergency."

"Oh." Felicity Fischer seemed disappointed.

"Then I gained the trust of her family, and here we are." Cray gave the machine a triumphant pat.

"Gracious, Bertie," Felicity Fischer applauded. "I thought you were the stupid one of the family."

"Do you want to know the best bit?" Cray boasted. "Mr Snook, my boss, thinks Dr Plunket stole it! He's after her, not me."

Felicity Fischer frowned. "That's all very well," she said. "But why have you brought it to *me*? Why would you think *I'd* have a use for a rewilding machine?"

"Don't you *see*?" Cray gave a skip. "The *possibilities*."

Felicity Fischer stared at him. "Which *are*?"

Cray held up my rucksack. "On a separate, unplanned trip, I acquired a fine selection of DNA. I have sabre-toothed cats in here! Golden toads! Warty pigs! You could bring back prehistoric beasts!"

Felicity Fischer yawned. "There was a film about that," she said. "I don't think it ended well."

"OK, then." Cray moved swiftly on. "Handbags and hats!"

"Handbags and hats?" Felicity Fischer stared at him.

"Yes." Cray flung his arms out. "You've already got the factory. Can you imagine!" He struck a pose. "A sabre-toothed tote! A giant-beaver bonnet! People would pay a fortune!"

"Oh, for goodness' sake," Felicity Fischer snapped. "I'm not Cruella de Vil. Disappointing as it *is*, people don't *want* to wear dead animals any more."

"They still eat them. How about steak?" Cray was starting to sweat. "Mammoth steak? I mean, *yummy*. I bet there's a market for mammoth steak?"

Felicity Fischer sighed. "There would have been," she said, "if it wasn't for the vegans. Dreadful things. They'd make a terrible fuss. The world's gone crazy, Bertie. People are milking *nuts*." She gave a shudder. "I'm afraid, dear cousin, your machine is worth diddly-squat to me. You may as well pop it back where you found it."

Cray jumped to his feet. "Youth!" he shouted desperately. "Beauty!"

Felicity Fischer stopped. "What do you mean?" she asked.

"You could mix your genes with those from someone younger," Cray gabbled. "It'd work a treat."

Felicity Fischer stared at him in fury. "What *are* you implying?"

Cray backtracked. "Not *you*," he said. "I was thinking of … um … *aging pop stars*. They'd pay a fortune!"

Felicity Fischer narrowed her eyes. "Maybe," she said. She peered closely at him. "I can see you haven't tried it." She gave a snigger.

"No," Cray admitted. "Though I did accidentally turn myself into a rat."

Felicity Fischer's eyebrows shot up. "Did you?" she said.

Cray nodded. "I was exactly the same inside, I was just a rat on the outside."

"Is that so?" Felicity Fischer looked thoughtful.

"Yes!" Cray said, excitedly. "And it's easy to turn yourself back. I mean, you could rent the machine out for fancy dress parties! Imagine going along to one as a real live hippo, or a giraffe! You'd win first prize every time."

"Well, that's absolutely *genius*," Felicity Fischer said. "I can see I'm going to make a lot of money from that, Bertie."

"Really?" Cray looked at her eagerly.

Felicity Fischer tutted loudly. "I was mocking you, Bertie. It's a *ridiculous* idea."

"Oh." Cray looked deflated.

Felicity Fischer placed a consoling hand on his shoulder. "I could probably find *some* use for it. How much do you want?"

Cray gave an excited squeal. "Well, there's the machine and the blueprints and the DNA – and I purchased these fine chickens from a neighbour so you could experiment." He thought for a moment. "How about three million – and I'll throw in the rats and a hamster?"

"Three million?" Felicity

Fischer's eyebrows vanished into her hair. "Oh, dear me, no. I'll give you what it's worth." She reached into her pocket and pulled out some notes. "Here you go."

Cray took the money and stared at it. "What's this?" he said.

"Twenty-five pounds." Felicity Fischer picked up Mum's machine and popped it on the trolley. "Do you need a receipt?"

"Twenty-five pounds?" Cray blinked. "That's a joke, right?"

"Not at all," Felicity Fischer said. She swung the trolley round and headed for a door marked EXECUTIVE EXIT TO CAR PARK.

"You stop right there!" Cray scurried after her. "I'll give you the twenty-five pounds back and sell my machine to someone else!"

Felicity Fischer didn't stop. "It's not your machine," she chortled. "It's mine."

"It isn't." Cray caught up and grabbed the machine from the trolley. Felicity Fischer snatched it back, then kicked him in the ankle. "Hands off, you toad!" she snapped.

"I'll tell on you," Cray screeched. "I'll go back to the lab and tell them you've got it. You'll go to jail for receiving stolen goods."

"No, I won't, Bertie." Felicity Fischer gave a snort. "And do you know why? They won't believe you because you're a LOSER, while I am extremely rich and very important."

"I am NOT a loser." Cray made another attempt to grab the machine.

Felicity Fischer tripped him. "You are, and you always will be. I only gave you a job because your brother asked me to, and you were useless at that."

"I wasn't." Cray scrambled to his feet.

"Yes, you were. That's why I fired you." Felicity Fischer ran over his foot with the trolley.

"OW!" Dr Cray hopped around in pain.

Felicity Fischer giggled. "See? A total loser. Now buzz off and don't come back."

She rammed the trolley into the door to the car park

and it flew open. She trundled through it with a wave.

"See ya."

Cray stared wordlessly after her.

Then he started to cry.

EIGHTEEN

We cautiously came out of hiding and made our way over to the sobbing Cray.

"There, there." Penny patted his shoulder. "Have a tissue." She rummaged through her pocket and pulled one out.

"Thank you." Cray blew his nose loudly.

I stared at Penny. "What are you doing?" I hissed. "Did you not hear? He planned to steal the machine all along!"

"We need his help to get it back," she muttered. "Be nice."

Be *nice*? Was she kidding? After what he'd done?

Penny turned back to Cray. "I heard what Felicity Fischer said. You were the *honest* one. You never even cheated at cards. I expect this was just a one-off, wasn't it?"

Cray nodded dolefully. "I just wanted some money. Everyone's successful apart from me. My brother's the prime minister and Felicity has five Lamborghinis." He blew his nose loudly. "I always wanted a Lamborghini."

"I want an Xbox," I said, "but I don't go round stealing stuff."

Penny stepped on my foot. "What you have to remember, Cray, is the best things in life are free."

"Lamborghinis aren't," Cray howled.

"Lamborghinis are *terrible* for the environment," Penny said. "And there are LOADS of things that are better than money. Dogs, for a start. And friends."

"I don't have any friends," Cray wailed. "No one likes me."

"I didn't say it was easy," Penny said. "Sometimes you have to make an effort. Invite people over to tea. Join a club."

"Stop stealing stuff?" I suggested. "Ow."

Penny had stepped on my foot again. "In the meantime, Percy and I will be your friends, won't we, Percy?"

She elbowed me in the ribs.

"*Love* to," I said.

"You will?" Cray looked up joyfully. "After everything I've done?"

Penny nodded. "But you'll have to help us get the machine back. Can we use your van to follow Felicity Fischer?"

Cray bounded to his feet. "Of course!"

I went and got the trolley with Chip on and we wheeled it towards the exit. "Why do you think she even wants the machine?" I asked. "She didn't seem interested in anything it could do."

"I *know*," Cray complained.

"I *liked* your fancy dress idea," Penny said.

"It *was* good, wasn't it?" Cray said.

There was a slight hiccup in the car park.

There was no sign of Cray's van.

"Where's it gone?" Cray looked around in panic.

"Felicity Fischer must have taken it," I said. "I don't expect she could get the boxes in the boot of her Lamborghini."

Cray gave a little squeal. "She's left her Lamborghini. Oh *joy*!" He raced across to it and around to the driver's side. He pulled open the door. "The keys are in it!" he crowed. "Oh happy, *happy* day!" He did a little dance. "Come on, come on! All aboard!" He hopped inside.

"Is there room?" Penny looked doubtful. "It's ever so small."

"They're not the most practical cars," Cray admitted. "But they are the very *finest*." He patted the steering wheel. "This must be the fastest car in Great Potton. I've *always* wanted to drive one." He turned the key and the engine started with a throaty roar.

Penny crammed herself into the tiny back seat with Chip, and I strapped myself into the front. Cray turned on the lights and stepped on the gas.

The car lurched, then stalled.

"Whoops!" Cray gave a giggle. He started the

engine again, and this time we crept forward. "Isn't it *amazing?*" he said.

I held my breath and waited for the car to pick up speed.

Cray edged out of the gates.

I looked back at the walls of Felicity Fischer's factory. "You didn't see my dad on the way in, did you?" I asked.

"I don't think so." Cray changed gear with a clunk. "What was he wearing?"

"Nothing," I said.

"Sorry?"

"Nothing," I said. "Don't worry. I'm sure he's fine."

NINETEEN

It wasn't far to Felicity Fischer's mansion, but Cray drove the fastest car in Great Potton very slowly. At every junction he took ages to pull out, even if there was no traffic. At one point I suggested he hurry up, but he got cross and asked if I *wanted* him to crash. "This is a powerful beast!" he snapped. "It needs to be treated with respect."

"My grandma drives faster," Penny said.

Cray turned to scowl at her and almost left the road.

I watched him as he drove. "Cray," I said, "you know the chickens?"

Cray sniffed. "The ones Felicity took?"

"Yes. You said you bought them from a neighbour. Was that true?"

He nodded.

"Which neighbour?"

"The really old one," Cray said. "Mrs Miggins, I think her name was."

"You're sure?

"Yes," Cray huffed. "Ten pounds each, she charged. Extortionate, but I needed some creatures to experiment with, so I bought two. I got the rats from the lab and Gertie from the pet shop at the retail park."

"No guinea pigs then?" I asked, casually.

Dr Cray shook his head. "No."

I frowned. It *sounded* like he was telling the truth, but Mrs Miggins had *definitely* told the newspapers her chickens were stolen.

It was very odd.

"Turn left at the Co-op," Penny said. "That's it. Here."

We edged through enormous wrought iron gates and on to Felicity Fischer's tree-lined drive. Off the

162

main road, Cray was a little braver. I watched as the needle on the speedometer crept up. Cray looked at me. "Too fast?"

"Absolutely not," I said.

Penny suggested he turn the lights off. "We're nearly at the house," she said. "We don't want to be spotted."

"Good idea," Cray agreed. He looked for the button and immediately veered on to the grass. The Lamborghini took out two small saplings and a statue, before coming to rest in a hedge.

"What *excellent* parking," I said. "And so clever of you. Felicity Fischer will never see the car here."

Cray beamed at me. "I didn't *intend* to leave the road," he confessed, "but once I had, I saw this would be an ideal place to conceal ourselves." He scrambled out and gave the Lamborghini a pat. "A wonderful piece of machinery," he said.

I pulled Penny and a sleeping Chip out of the back. I'd suggested we leave him in the car, but Penny didn't want to. "If he wakes up, he'll have no idea where he is." She gave Chip an anxious look. "Do you think we gave him too much of that stress remedy, Cray?"

"All natural ingredients, Penny. Completely harmless. I expect he'll wake up any minute, all refreshed." Cray gave Chip a pat. "Let me take him for a while?"

"That's kind of you," Penny said. She handed the holdall over.

"Gracious." Cray almost dropped it. "He is rather heavy, isn't he?" He looked at me hopefully.

There was no way I was offering to carry Chip!

164

I headed after Penny before he could ask. She was peering around the hedge towards Felicity Fischer's mansion. "It's *huge*," she whispered.

I stood next to her and stared. That wasn't a house, it was a *palace*. It had turrets and balconies and a giant portico, and a whole load of bushes cut into fancy shapes. In the middle of the forecourt, a fountain was sending up jets of water in time to an energetic polka.

The whole place blazed with light.

"Where's Cray?" Penny asked.

I turned and watched him struggle towards us. "He's coming," I said.

"Do you think we can trust him?" Penny asked.

I stared at her. "No," I said. "Of course not. Do you?"

Penny shrugged. "He might genuinely be sorry," she said. "But we should keep an eye on him."

"Yes," I said. "We jolly well *should*."

Cray staggered up beside us. He put Chip down and wiped his brow. "What's the plan?"

"I was hoping you could help with that," Penny said. "You said you used to work here. How do we get in?"

"We'll sneak in the back." Cray pointed across the grass. "It's this way."

"Wait!" hissed Penny. "I hear a car!"

She was right. We ducked down behind a hydrangea as a set of headlights swept up the drive. They swung around the fountain and came to a halt outside the entrance.

"That's Mr Snook!" I said.

"Mr Snook?" Cray spluttered. "Why would *he* be here?"

"Does he know Felicity Fischer?" I asked.

"I guess he must," Cray sniffed. "Though I didn't know."

"Do you think she's going to give him the machine back?" Penny asked.

Cray snorted. "I expect she'll *sell* it back to him," he said, bitterly. "For a *lot* more than twenty-five pounds. And she'll tell him I took it and I'll get the sack."

We watched as Mr Snook climbed out the driver's seat and trotted up the steps, smoothing back his hair and brushing his lapels.

He rapped loudly and, after a second or two, the door swung open.

"It's Felicity," whispered Cray.

There was a murmur of voices and Mr Snook stepped inside. The door slammed shut behind him.

The fountain began to play a brisk foxtrot.

"Let's go," Cray said.

TWENTY

We followed Cray across the grass to the back of the house.

"There's your van, Cray!" Penny ran over and peered through the window. "The keys are in the ignition!" She pulled open the door. "It's not locked."

I ran over to look in the back, but it was empty.

"She'll have taken everything in," Cray said. "We'd better hurry."

"Which way?"

"Through that arch." He pointed.

The arch led to a small courtyard. Cray put the

169

holdall down and rubbed his shoulder. "This is the servants' entrance," he said.

"Does Felicity Fischer have *servants*?" Penny asked.

Cray shook his head. "Not since she fired me." He nodded towards a door. "I left a key under that mat."

I went over and lifted it up. "I can't see one," I said.

Cray came over to check. "Drat," he said. "She's moved it."

"How do we get in, then?" I asked. "Is there another way?"

Cray looked sly. "There's always the drains?"

I stared at him, coldly. "I think *not*," I said.

"Do tell me your better plan." Cray gave a little bow.

Luckily, I was saved by an extra loud snort from the holdall. Penny shrieked in delight. "Chip's waking up!" she said.

And that gave *her* an idea.

It took us a while, but we finally shook Chip completely awake and balanced him on his wobbly legs. He eyed me with fury. It seemed that the seven-hour sleep had not improved his mood.

"Go and sit in front of the door, Percy," Penny said.

"Why me?" I objected. "Why not Cray?"

"Chip doesn't like you. He'll charge faster."

She had a point. I grudgingly went and sat.

"It might take several goes," Cray chortled.

I wasn't doing this more than once! Bait. That's all I was: bait.

Penny held Chip tightly. He was still a bit unsteady, but his eyes were fixed on me. He pawed the ground and snorted furiously.

Penny looked up at me. "Wait till the last second before you dive out of the way, OK?"

I wiped away a bead of sweat. "OK," I said.

Chip sensed my fear. His nostrils flared and his tail twitched.

"Goad him, Percy," Penny shouted.

Goad him? I didn't need to *goad* him! Just me sitting there was doing the trick.

"Ready?" Penny shouted.

I answered with a panicked squeak.

She let go.

Chip charged.

I could barely breathe as he thundered towards me. I focused on his rapidly approaching horn. If I didn't get the timing right, I could die.

Five metres.

Four metres.

Three metres.

Two— Oh.

Was it my imagination, or had the thundering of Chip's hooves become more of a clippety-clop?

Or even just a clop.

I watched as he veered off course, crashed through some flowerpots and toppled over. He lay there for a moment, then gave a gentle snore.

Cray peered at him. "We must work on the dosage," he said. "I think six drops was too much."

"I might have poured a bit extra in," I muttered. "Sorry."

Penny stared at me. "How much extra?"

I stood up. "Not that mu—" I caught my foot on the mat and stumbled back against the door.

And fell inside.

It wasn't even locked.

TWENTY-ONE

We didn't take Chip into the house with us. Penny wanted to bring him, but I said that if we had to make a quick exit he'd slow us down, and then we'd *all* be caught. We put him in the van to finish his sleep, and then we went back to the house and crept inside.

"We just need to find the machine, grab it and run," I said. I strode off down the passage.

"You're going in the wrong direction," Cray called. "As I am familiar with the house, perhaps *I* should lead the way?"

I sheepishly came back.

"It's down here." Cray trotted down a corridor.

"What did you do when you worked for Felicity Fischer?" Penny jogged to keep up.

"I was the butler," Cray boasted. Then he paused. "I mainly answered the door."

"Is that it?" I said.

Cray shrugged. "Sometimes I had to take Felicity Fischer her post on a tray. And if she had anyone important staying, I had to eavesdrop."

"What for?" Penny asked.

"To get information, of course," Cray said. "In case she needed to blackmail anyone."

"Blackmail?" Penny's mouth fell open. "That's *awful*."

"Did you ever hear anything good?" I asked.

"No," Cray said. "That's why she fired me." He gave an injured sniff. "I was left without a penny. A life of crime seemed the only way."

"Well, now you know it *isn't*," Penny said.

We followed Cray up some stairs and along a corridor that seemed to go on for *ever*. The carpet was really deep, which made it hard to walk, and every now and then there was an alcove with a statue in it. It must be weird to live in a house this big. Weird – and *tiring*. "Are we almost there?" I asked.

Cray nodded. "They'll be in the sitting room," he said. "It's off the great hall." He stopped with a grand gesture. "Which is here."

Blimey. Most people's halls are narrow and full of coats and wellingtons, but this one was enormous and had a domed ceiling with pictures all over it. In the middle, a huge staircase swept up to the floors above.

"This is bigger than my whole house." Penny looked around in awe.

"I can hear voices," I whispered.

"Over there." Cray pointed across the hall to a door that was ajar.

I tiptoed over and peered through the gap. Wow. The sitting room was as big as the hall. It was stuffed full of fancy furniture and ornaments and over by the window were Cray's boxes, with Gertie's cage and my rucksack perched on top. There was no sign of Mum's machine.

Felicity Fischer and Mr Snook were standing by the fireplace, chatting. I tried to hear what they were saying, but I couldn't. I went back to the others. "I'll have to get closer," I said. "I'll crawl in and hide behind that sofa."

"I'll come with you," Penny said.

Cray gave an excited hop. "I'll go and get the van. I'll bring it round and wait by the fountain with the engine running. As soon as you have the machine, escape out the front. We can make a quick getaway." He headed for the door.

I stared after him. It *sounded* like a good plan.

The door banged behind him.

"Hey!" Penny said. "How do we know he's not going to disappear?"

"We don't," I said.

TWENTY-TWO

We inched through the door and across to an armchair. From there, we darted to a sideboard, then over to a large sofa. We squeezed behind it and slithered along, then I very slowly and carefully stuck my head out.

Felicity Fischer had poured Mr Snook some lemonade. She handed it to him, then gestured to a fancy table. "It's been *lovely* hearing about your holiday in Bognor Regis," she said, "but let's get down to business, shall we?"

Mr Snook took a seat.

Felicity Fischer sat down opposite. "First, I must

thank you for popping over at such short notice," she said. She gave him a warm smile.

"I was rather surprised to get your call." Mr Snook took a nervous sip of his drink.

"I just wondered how things were going at the lab?" Felicity Fischer leant back in her chair and gazed at him. "All good?"

Mr Snook nodded vigorously. "Everything's going *wonderfully*," he said.

"That's good to hear." Felicity Fischer beamed at him. "Nothing interesting to report?"

"No." Mr Snook gazed nonchalantly out the window. "Nothing at all."

"No inventions I might be interested in?" Felicity Fischer probed.

Mr Snook swallowed. "Nope," he said.

Felicity Fischer narrowed her eyes. "Sure?"

"Absolutely." Mr Snook wiped a bead of sweat from his brow.

Felicity Fischer pulled Mum's machine from a bag. She plonked it on the table.

Mr Snook's jaw dropped. "How did you get that?" he squawked. "I thought Dr Plunket had stolen it."

"My cousin Bertie dropped it off," Felicity Fischer said. "Seems the security at your lab is rubbish." She leant over and poked Mr Snook in the chest. "Did you forget about our deal? I fund the institute and get first dibs on anything you invent. You're supposed tell me everything that goes on."

Mr Snook mopped his forehead. "I didn't think you'd be interested in a rewilding machine."

"Not interested?" Felicity Fischer thumped the table. "Why wouldn't I be interested?" She sat back in her chair. "I have big plans for it."

Mr Snook looked confused. "You have? But you're the least green person I know!"

"You're absolutely right," Felicity Fischer nodded. "And until that awful Hetta Bunberg came along, everyone was perfectly happy with the delights of single-use plastics." She gave a deep scowl. "Now, however, you can't move for protesters. They're denting my profits." She patted the machine "That's why I need this."

"What for?" Mr Snook asked.

Felicity Fischer puffed herself up. "I'm going to announce an incredible rewilding programme, the likes of which have never been seen before! People will think I'm marvellous! They'll be so busy admiring my dodos they'll forget about my plastic bag factory, or the fact I plan to tarmac over the park for my space programme."

Mr Snook looked horrified. "But you can't bring animals back *yet*. The planet's not ready. They'll die out again."

Felicity Fischer rolled her eyes. "They're only *animals*, Mr Snook. It doesn't matter if they're temporary."

Mr Snook stood his ground. "It's not ethical. I can't let you."

Felicity Fischer shrugged. "You don't have a choice," she said, nastily. "Without my cash, your institute will go bust. This isn't your only project. It's in your interests to keep me on side."

Mr Snook finally crumpled. "What will I tell Dr

Plunket?" he asked. "She's been working on it for *years.*"

"You'll think of something." Felicity Fischer gave a dainty yawn. *"Though"* – she sat forward excitedly – "if she's got nothing else to do, she could build a spaceship for me. One big enough to take fifty billionaires into space!"

Mr Snook jumped up. "I think I should be going," he said.

"Wait!" Felicity Fischer jumped up too. She patted the machine. "My cousin didn't bring any instructions. I need you to show me how this works."

Mr Snook took a step back. "It's not been properly tested yet."

"Don't worry! Bertie tried it out!" Felicity Fischer gave an excited clap. "He said it worked perfectly – but I'd like to see for myself." She pointed over at Cray's boxes. "I have everything we need. Chickens, rats, a hamster … and *these.*" She reached back into the bag and pulled out a handful of tubs. "From your lab, no less. A wonderful selection." She held them up and read out the labels. "Two-toed sloth! Mammoth! Elephant shrew!" She paused. "What shall we bring back first?"

"It really isn't a good idea," Mr Snook snapped.

"Don't be a spoilsport. We'll do something small." She pointed over to Gertie's cage. "Get me that fat little hamster."

"No." Mr Snook headed for the door. "I want no part in this."

"Come back!" Felicity Fischer shouted.

"Absolutely *not!*" Mr Snook squawked.

"Well don't expect a cut of my profits!" Felicity Fischer yelled after him.

"I never would!" he yelled back.

The door crashed shut.

Felicity Fischer scowled after him, purple-faced. "Such a goody-goody," she muttered. "I don't need him. I'll work it out for myself." She stomped over to Gertie's cage and poked around in the bedding. There was a small amount of rustling before Felicity Fischer screeched "GOT YOU," followed by "OW!"

In that same second, Gertie leapt from her hand.

I squeaked in horror as the hamster flew through the air.

Luckily, she landed on one of the armchairs.

"Come here." An enraged Felicity Fischer grabbed at her. "I'll teach you to bite me."

Gertie didn't want a lesson in not biting. She clambered down the upholstery and scampered across the floor. Felicity Fischer made a dive, but Gertie was too quick.

We watched, powerless, as she made a beeline for the sofa we were hiding behind.

Followed closely by Felicity Fischer.

I turned to try and wiggle out, but Penny was in the way.

Bum.

This wasn't in the plan.

TWENTY-THREE

Felicity Fischer was absolutely LIVID when she saw us.

Apoplectic.

Furious.

COMPLETELY PUCE.

"Who are you?" she bellowed.

Penny and I slunk out and stood in front of her. "I'm Percy," I said.

"I'm Penny," said Penny, politely. "Hi."

Introductions did nothing for Felicity Fischer's mood. She looked like she was going to explode any minute. "What are you doing in my sitting room?" she screeched.

"We were helping you look for the hamster," Penny

said. "We came in and could see you'd lost it, so that's what we were doing behind the sofa."

"What rubbish," Felicity Fischer snapped.

"It's true." I nodded vigorously. "That's what we were doing."

"Nothing worse than losing a pet," Penny commiserated.

"I can think of *plenty* of worse things." Felicity Fischer narrowed her eyes.

"I *completely* see we shouldn't have let ourselves in," Penny said, "but that man left the door open."

"Snook? He's an idiot," Felicity Fischer raged. "Why are you here? Did that no-good cousin of mine send you to get the machine back?"

Penny wasn't used to her charm not working. She faltered under Felicity Fischer's gaze. "We ... um..."

I took charge. "You're right," I said. "Bertie did send us."

"I knew it!" Felicity Fischer screeched. "The weasel."

"He said he'd forgotten to give you these." I pulled the instructions for Mum's machine from my pocket.

188

"He'd like you to have them, with his apologies for his rudeness earlier."

Felicity Fischer looked mighty suspicious, but she snatched the notebook anyway. Her face became less purple as she flicked through it.

"Gracious," she muttered. "He must be trying to wheedle his way into my good books."

Penny had pulled me to one side. "Why did you give her those?" she whispered.

"I'm integrating myself," I whispered back. "I think it's worked."

It had. Felicity Fischer closed the notebook with a snap. She beamed over at us. "I expect Bertie told you about the machine," she said. "I was about to try it out. Would you two like to help?"

"That would be really great," I said.

"I just need to find that horrible hamster." Felicity Fischer picked up a cushion and checked underneath. "You two can help me look."

"Of course," I said. I peered under a chair.

"What's the plan?" Penny muttered in my ear.

"We go along with whatever she asks," I muttered back. "Then, when she's least expecting it, we'll grab Mum's machine and run."

Penny raised her eyebrows. "So the same plan as before, then?"

I scowled at her. "Unless you have a better one?"

"Not at the moment." She dived behind a chest and reappeared with Gertie.

"You've got her!" I stared in delight.

Penny tucked Gertie into her pocket. "Don't say anything. I'm not letting that old bat blend her genes."

"Any luck?" Felicity Fischer called over.

"No," Penny lied. "Not a whisker."

Felicity Fischer scowled. "We've looked long enough. We'll use a chicken instead." She pointed to Dr Cray's boxes. "Could you fetch one?"

"Of course," I said politely.

We wrestled one out and carried it to the table.

"Thank you." Felicity Fischer smiled fondly at us. "Isn't this exciting! Make sure you tell all your little school friends about my green credentials, won't you?"

"Your what?" I asked.

"My green credentials. That I truly have the environment at heart." Felicity Fischer smoothed back her curls. "That I have put body and soul into bringing all these poor dear animals back."

"Right," I said.

"Body and soul – and an *awful* lot of cash," Felicity Fischer prattled on. "Still, you have to spend money to make money. I could come and do a school assembly, if you like?"

"That would be wonderful," Penny said, politely.

"What shall we do first?" Felicity Fischer rummaged eagerly through the tubs. "How about a two-toed sloth? Or an elephant shrew? No." She seized another. "Let's do a broad-billed parrot. I do *love* a parrot."

Mum's machine worked exactly as it should. The bird soared above our heads in a flash of brightly coloured feathers. Every now and then it surprised itself with a cluck. Felicity Fischer was thrilled. "Isn't it MARVELLOUS?" she crowed. "My greenwashing – I mean, *rewilding* – programme is going to be SUCH a success!"

The parrot was glorious. I watched as it landed on the curtain pole and comically sidled along it. I felt outraged on its behalf. How could people let something so amazing go extinct?

"What shall we do next?" Felicity Fischer dug around in my rucksack. "Shall we use the other chicken, or one of the rats? Did Bertie bring me any dodo DNA? Prep the machine, Percy."

"OK," I said. I looked at Penny. "Ready?" I whispered.

She nodded.

"NOW!"

I grabbed the machine from the table. At the same time, Penny snatched the rucksack from Felicity Fischer's hands.

We hurtled across the room.

We ran as fast as we could, but it wasn't any use.

We didn't even make it to the door.

TWENTY-FOUR

Felicity Fischer had us by our dungaree straps. "Ha," she sniggered. "Didn't know I was the Great Potton cross-country champion 1986, did you? In my *prime*, I was. Barely had to cheat." She gave us a shake, then marched us back to the table. "Put my machine down," she ordered.

"It's not yours," I said, though I did as she said. "It's my mum's."

Felicity Fischer's eyebrows shot up. "Dr Plunket? She's your mother?" She gave a giggle. "Well, well, well."

"Well, well, well, *what*?" I scowled at her.

"That must mean your father is *Mr* Plunket."

"Yes." I pulled myself free of her grip. "What about it?"

Felicity Fischer gave a smirk. "We don't get on."

"You don't say," I said.

"In fact," she continued, "I'd go as far as to say Mr Plunket is the *bane* of my life."

"What's a bane?" Penny asked.

"A PAIN IN THE BUTT!" Felicity Fischer gave a ferocious scowl. "Everywhere I looked, *there* he was. If he wasn't protesting about my plastic bags, he was ferreting around at the council for information to use against me. I knew that the *second* he found out about my plan to tarmac the park he'd never let up. Something had to be done."

"What do you mean?" I said.

Felicity Fischer thumped the table. "I had to stop him."

I thought of Dad's bag in the skip. My insides went cold. "What did you do?" I whispered.

Felicity Fischer giggled. "I started a rumour. I said the prime minister was going to visit my factory, and that I was going to announce some 'new environmental policies'. I *knew* your father wouldn't be able to resist."

"You laid a trap?" Penny said.

Felicity Fischer nodded. "Up he turned, him and his elderly friend, ready to denounce me. I was lying in wait." She paused for a moment. "I was a little surprised it was a *naked* protest, but I averted my gaze and kept my nerve."

I swallowed hard. What had she done?

"I'd hired a Portaloo especially for the occasion. I locked them in it. They were *furious*." She gave a satisfied smile. "I used the Lamborghini to tow it here, then tipped them into the cellar. I hadn't *quite* decided what to do with them, so I went back to the factory to have a think. When Bertie brought me the machine, it gave me the most wonderful idea!"

"What was it?" I asked.

Felicity Fischer didn't reply. She bent down and pulled at a ring embedded in a flagstone. It flew up to reveal an opening in the floor.

A set of rickety steps led into darkness.

"You can come out now," Felicity Fischer bellowed down them.

I stared at her. "Is that where Dad is?" I asked.

"Percy? Is that you?" Dad's head popped out of the opening. "What are you doing here?"

I didn't think it was the best time to explain about turning Chip into a rhino. "I'll tell you later," I said.

Dad clambered up the rest of the ladder and scrambled out, closely followed by Mrs Miggins. I was relieved to see she'd lent Dad her poncho.

"All OK?" Felicity Fischer asked politely.

"No thanks to you. You took the bag with the sandwiches," Mrs Miggins huffed. "I'm starving."

"More importantly, you *ruined* my demonstration." Dad snapped.

Felicity Fischer held up her hand. "Mr Plunket,"

she said, "I can only apologize for earlier. I got carried away. I think the time has come for us to sit around the table and sort things out, like grown-ups. I've got some *lovely* biscuits." She reached for a tin on the side.

"Biscuits?" Mrs Miggins sat down immediately.

Dad didn't look particularly keen on sorting things out like grown-ups, but he grudgingly sat next to Mrs Miggins.

It was only then that he noticed the gene blender. He gawped at it for a moment, then gave me an accusing stare.

I gazed out the window.

"Sit down, Penny." Felicity Fischer bustled over with a tin of biscuits. "And you too, Percy."

We did as she said. It wasn't like we had a choice.

We couldn't leave without Mum's machine.

"Do you think Cray is still outside?" Penny whispered in my ear.

"Hope so," I muttered back.

Felicity Fischer didn't sit down herself. She offered

round the biscuits and poured everyone a glass of lemonade. "All comfy?" she asked.

I wasn't sure if we were supposed to reply or not, so I just nodded.

"Good, good." Felicity Fischer gave a little giggle. "*First,*" she said. "I'd like to congratulate Mr Plunket for the *very* fine glue he brought along to the protest. I borrowed a jar from his bag, and while you weren't looking just now, I tipped a little on each seat."

Dad's mouth dropped open. He tried to jump up, but he couldn't.

I tried to pull myself free, and so did Penny and Mrs Miggins, but it really was *excellent* glue.

We were stuck fast.

It wasn't a good feeling.

"As none of you are rushing off," Felicity Fischer chortled. "Who'd like to hear my amazingly brilliant idea?"

"Not me." Dad scowled at her.

"Rude." Felicity Fischer stamped her foot. "I shall tell you anyway."

Dad pretended to yawn, but it didn't put Felicity Fischer off. "As you know," she began, "I am a hugely successful business person."

"A hugely *corrupt* one, you mean," squawked Mrs Miggins, through a mouthful of custard cream.

Felicity Fischer took no notice and carried on. "Sadly, I've noted that certain ... um... less *green* aspects of my work are attracting unwanted attention." She gave Dad an unfriendly stare. "It's affecting my profits and needs to stop."

Dad snorted. "I'll never stop," he said. *"Never."*

"And *that*" – Felicity Fischer gave him a wide and toothy smile – "is exactly why you ended up in my cellar. If it hadn't been for my dear cousin delivering this machine, I'd have left you to starve."

"Starve?" I stared at her in horror. "You wouldn't have, would you?"

Felicity Fischer smirked. "Why not? No one knew they were there."

"That would be *murder.*" Penny looked shocked.

"But there was so much at stake!" Felicity Fischer

cried. "My factory, my space programme, my retirement fund. What choice did I have?" She beamed around at us. "Now, you'll be pleased to hear that thanks to this..." She leant forward and patted the machine. "Murder is off the table."

Thank goodness for that. I relaxed.

"Instead," Felicity Fischer crowed, "I'm going to turn you all into mice."

TWENTY-FIVE

There was a stunned silence from everyone but Mrs Miggins, who was rummaging for a pink wafer.

"You're what?" I said. I forgot about the glue and tried to stand up. "You're going to do *what*?"

"Turn you into *mice*." Felicity Fischer held up a tub. "Galapagos mice, to be precise. Dear little things, all fat and fluffy according to the picture on the lid. Believed to have gone extinct in 1930 or so." She put the tub down and beamed. "And *then*, I shall ... um ... *rewild* you."

"*Rewild* us?" Penny shrieked.

"Yes. Set you free. Isn't that *lovely* of me?" Felicity Fischer clasped her hands and gave a beatific smile.

"You can't do that," I said. "We'll be eaten by a fox or … or … an owl or something."

Felicity Fischer pulled a sad face. "That would be *terrible* – but perfectly *natural*. Survival of the fittest. *Super* eco-friendly. My conscience will be clear." She scooped some DNA out of the tub and popped it in the drawer. "Who'd like to go first?"

Dad tried to free himself but couldn't. He scowled instead. "You win, Fischer," he said. "I'll never protest about anything you do *ever* again – not even your space programme."

"Really?" Felicity Fischer paused.

"Yes." Dad nodded vigorously. "I promise."

"I don't believe you." She picked up the cables and waved them at him. "I'm afraid this is the only way."

"At least let Percy and Penny go," Dad pleaded.

"I'm afraid I have to do *all* of you, or someone will grass me up. We can't have that." Felicity Fischer looked around the table. "Now—"

I could only see one way out of this.

It might not work.

But I had to try.

I put my hand up. "I'll go first," I said.

"*No*, Percy," Dad shook his head. "Let me."

"It's fine, Dad," I said. "Honestly."

"Are you sure?" Penny looked like she might be sick.

"I have a plan," I whispered.

That didn't seem to reassure her. "I hope it's better than the last one," she whispered back.

Felicity Fischer trotted up behind me, "Ready?" she said. "One on each ear, is it?"

"I don't think it *has* to be the ears," I said. "Just wherever's easiest."

She gave a giggle. "Yours stick out so nicely. It'd be silly not to. You'll make a lovely mouse." She clipped the cables on, then reached for the machine. She frowned. "Which button was it again?" she asked.

"It's not a button," I said. "You turn the dial."

"Oh yes. I remember now." She twisted it all the way round.

"Everyone should shut their eyes," I said.

"Of course. Thank you, Percy." Felicity Fischer closed hers.

I concentrated on the tick.

If this was going to work, I had to get the timing *exactly* right.

Tick.

Tick.

Tick.

Tick.

Tick.

NOW!

I pulled the clips from my ears and snapped them on to Felicity Fischer's.

Ping!

There was a flash and a sizzling and a terrible, *terrible* smell.

I hadn't had time to shut my own eyes. I blinked and blinked until I could see again.

When I *could*, the first thing I looked for was a dear little Galapagos mouse running around the table.

Strange. I couldn't *see* a Galapagos mouse. Come to

that, I couldn't see Mum's machine either. What I *could* see was Dad's horrified face as he stared at something behind me.

What I could *feel* was hot breath on my neck, accompanied by a deep and angry rumbling.

I turned.

Oh.

I immediately realized what must have happened: when Cray had knocked the tubs off the shelf in the lab, some of the lids had come off.

It seemed that when I'd screwed them back on I'd mixed them up.

In *particular*, it seemed that I'd screwed the lid from the tub of Galapagos mouse on to the tub of mammoth.

In pictures, mammoths look friendly. All fluffy and cute.

This one wasn't either of those. This one towered above me, all hair and teeth, enormous trunk swinging, tiny yellow eyes blazing. Mum's machine dangled from her ear like a fancy earring.

Things hadn't *quite* gone to plan, after all.

Felicity Fischer bellowed in my face.

If I hadn't been glued to the chair, the force of her breath would have hurled me off it.

She bellowed again, in pure rage.

I stared into her mighty jaws in awe. She could crush my head in one bite, if she wanted. Impale me on her massive tusks. Mash me with her mighty feet.

Luckily, Felicity Fischer was finding it hard to control her newly acquired trunk. She took an enraged swipe at me, but only caught the table. It flew across the room before smashing into the wall and splintering into a million bits of firewood.

She trumpeted in rage, then stood there, breathing heavily, a murderous glint in her eyes. I tried to wrench myself from the chair but it was no good. Dad's glue was too strong.

We were going to die, weren't we?

Murdered by a mammoth.

I should *never* have gone into the spare room.

I squeezed my eyes tight shut and waited.

"Percy!" Penny screamed. She reached over and

undid the clasps on my dungaree bib. "Leave them behind."

I moved like lightning. Before Felicity Fischer realized what was happening, I was out of my dungarees, and free. I dropped to the floor and scrambled through her legs.

Penny followed me, holding Gertie. *"Hurry!"* she yelled.

We ran full pelt towards the door.

Felicity Fischer wheeled about and thundered after us.

"Go Percy! Go Penny!" squealed Mrs Miggins.

"RUN!" shouted Dad.

TWENTY-SIX

I don't think I'd *ever* moved as fast. We dashed around the sofas and statues and reached the hall in seconds. I stopped at the foot of the stairs to take a breath.

"We're safe," I said. "She'll never get through that door."

Felicity Fischer proved me wrong, with a great splintering crash.

"We need to get to Cray!" Penny shouted as we hurled ourselves through the enormous front entrance and down the great stone steps. Felicity Fischer was on our heels but the pillars of the portico held her for a moment. She trumpeted in rage as she tried to get her shoulders free.

We ran down the steps and across to the fountain. "Where's the van?" I looked around in panic. "Penny, where is it?"

Penny stopped. She looked like she was going to cry. "He's gone," she said. "He's gone." She shook her head. "He couldn't be trusted after all."

"You're wrong!" I shouted. "Look!"

The van sped around the corner of the house. It careered gaily across the gravel towards us. "Who's that driving?" Penny asked.

I squinted, then blinked in surprise. "I think it's Mr Snook," I said.

It was! He slammed on the brakes with a great spray of gravel. "Get in," he screeched out the window at us.

"Hooray!" cheered Penny.

Cray flung open the passenger door and budged up.

"You've been ages," he complained as we scrambled in. "I was waiting like we agreed, then Mr Snook came over to see what I was doing. I explained everything and we decided to team up."

"You did?" I stared at them.

"As long as I get the machine back, we'll say no more about any of it." Mr Snook slammed the van into gear.

"Ah," I said.

"You have got it, haven't you?" Cray looked at me. "I told Amos you were bringing it."

I gulped. "I know that *was* the plan," I said. "But" – I nodded towards the portico – "it didn't go as smoothly as we hoped."

Mr Snook turned to look. His mouth dropped open, and then he gave a little squeak. "Is that a *mammoth*?" he said.

I nodded. "It's Felicity Fischer."

"Gracious!" Cray gave a snort of glee. "She must be furious!"

"Yes, she is." Penny handed me Gertie, then scrambled into the back with Chip. "If I were you, I'd get us out of here."

Mr Snook folded his arms. "I'm not leaving without the machine."

With a great bellow, Felicity Fischer wrenched herself free and thundered down the steps. She hurtled across the gravel towards us, trunk swinging, ears flapping, tusks glinting in the moonlight. Mum's machine was still attached to her ear, bobbing up and down. It was a horrible sight.

Mr Snook changed his mind. He stamped on the accelerator and spun the wheel. "She's after us!" He sounded panicked. "Which way?"

"Keep going around the fountain! She might get dizzy and career off into a bush," shouted Cray.

It was a good idea, but it was us who got dizzy, not Felicity Fischer.

"I'll take the drive instead," said Mr Snook.

I put Gertie in my pocket, then stuck my head out the window. "You'd better hurry. She's catching up."

I tried to think of the positives of our situation, but there was only one, and that was that Mr Snook was at the wheel and not Cray: we hung on tight as the van hurtled away from the house at a terrifying speed.

Cray had closed his eyes. "Gracious," he

murmured. "I'm not criticizing your driving, Amos, not in the *slightest* – but we do seem to be going rather fast."

Mr Snook looked in the mirror. "I'm afraid we have to," he said. "No one wrote anything down in the stone age. I had no idea how quick mammoths *were*."

"This one was cross-country champion in 1986," Penny said, helpfully. "She may not be representative."

We shot through the gates and on to the high street. It was a good thing it was so late – the Co-op had shut long ago and the pavements were dark and deserted. I checked behind us. "We're losing her," I said in relief.

Mr Snook took his foot off the gas.

"What are you doing?" I stared at him in panic. "I thought we were trying to escape!"

Mr Snook checked the mirror. "We can't have a mammoth charging around Great Potton," he said. "Once we've tired her out, we can corner her and decide what to do."

I thought of Felicity Fischer's jaws and tusks and

the fury in her eyes. "How exactly will we do the cornering?" I asked.

"I'm sure Amos has a plan." Cray looked at him expectantly.

"I'm afraid I don't," Mr Snook confessed.

"We could lure her to the park?" Penny suggested from the back. "The adventure fort's quite sturdy. We might be able to trap her in that!"

"Anyone got anything better?" Mr Snook asked hopefully.

Sadly, no one had.

"The park it is, then," he said. "Which way?"

"Go past the station." I said. I pointed ahead.

Then I gave a squeak of horror.

There, up in front of us, was a lone cyclist.

They were quite far away, but I immediately recognized the bike and its panniers, and the helmet, and the bag.

Penny saw my face. "Is that your *mum*?" she asked.

I gulped. "She must have been on the last train." I said. I turned to Mr Snook in panic. "We can't overtake her. If she sees a mammoth, she'll know it was something to do with me. We'll have to tell her everything."

"We don't want to do that," Mr Snook looked anxious. "Is there anywhere to turn off?"

"No," I said.

"OK then. Hold tight." He yanked up the handbrake. The van swung around with a squeal.

Felicity Fischer may have been surprised by our change of direction, but her stride never faltered.

She was coming straight at us.

Mr Snook stared through the windscreen in awe. "What an incredible creature! Can you imagine, Percy, what Great Potton was like before they went extinct? Great herds of these beasts roaming the land. Marvellous."

Cray mopped his brow. "Perhaps we could talk about that later?" he suggested, as the incredible creature thundered closer.

"Sorry." Mr Snook came to his senses and put his foot down.

"We're not going to *hit* her, are we?" Penny asked, as the van gathered speed.

"Of course not," Mr Snook sounded confident. "Any second now, she'll move to the side."

"Are you sure?" I said.

"Yes." Mr Snook pressed harder on the gas.

"I don't think she *is* going to," Penny said.

Penny was right. Felicity Fischer was going nowhere.

I stared in horror as we hurtled towards her swinging trunk and foaming jaws.

"Brace!" screeched Mr Snook.

We braced.

At the very last second, he spun the wheel. We shot up a steep bank, over a hedge and landed in a field.

Cray gazed at Mr Snook admiringly. "What remarkable driving," he said.

"Thanks." Mr Snook blushed.

"Can we save the compliments?" I snapped. "That hedge won't hold her for long."

There was a crash.

Penny looked in the mirror. "It hasn't held her at all," she said. "You'd better step on it."

Cray pointed to the corner of the field. "Head for that gate."

"Right." Mr Snook changed direction.

"One of us will have to jump out, fling it open, then jump back in once we're through," Cray said. "Percy? How do you feel about taking that role?"

I glared at him. "I'm not *quite* ready to die," I said.

"There's not time anyway. She's almost upon us." Mr Snook sped up.

We bumped across the grass. The gate was metres ahead.

Was he planning on smashing straight through? I checked my seat belt.

Cray clung to the door handle. "This van is hired, Amos," he said. "I'd prefer to not lose my deposit."

"I'll do my best." Mr Snook gripped the wheel hard.

And then he slammed on the brakes.

It wasn't as dramatic as it *could* have been as we

skidded a bit, but our stop was good enough for Felicity Fischer to be taken *completely* by surprise. She couldn't decelerate as fast as us. She hurtled past and crashed straight through the gate, across the road and head first into a thicket on the opposite bank.

"Hooray," cheered Penny.

Mr Snook stamped on the accelerator again. Before Felicity Fischer had time to reverse out, the van was through the opening and back on the road.

"That way." Cray pointed in the right direction.

"Thank you, Bertie." Mr Snook gave him a nod.

I stuck my head out the window again. "She's looking tired," I said.

"We're here," shouted Cray. "Great Potton Park. Turn left at the railings."

"Right you are." Mr Snook spun the van into the car park. "Where's the adventure fort?"

"You'd better slow down," Penny said. "There are speed bumps."

Her warning came too late.

The van shot into the air.

It landed nose first in a flower bed, before slowly thudding back down on its wheels.

"Oh dear," Mr Snook said.

We watched as Felicity Fischer turned in through the park gates.

She trumpeted in delight when she saw us.

We were done for.

TWENTY-SEVEN

Felicity Fischer thudded over to the smoking van. She poked her hairy trunk through the window and pulled us out one at a time. Then she took Cray by the scruff of his lab coat and held him high. "This is all your fault!" she bellowed. "Bringing me that stupid machine."

"You didn't *have* to buy it." Cray sniggered. "If you like, you can have a refund? I've still got your twenty-five pounds."

I stared in wonder. If I was that close to Felicity Fischer's mighty jaws, I wouldn't be winding her up.

Penny was waving frantically. "Felicity!" she shouted.

"The machine's still attached to your ear. If it drops off and breaks, you'll have to stay like that. *For ever.*"

"It's still attached?" Felicity Fischer froze. "Does that mean I can turn myself back? Which button is it?" She tried to look.

"You'll need someone to help," Penny said.

"I'll reset you." Cray said.

"You will?"

Cray giggled. "Yes. For three million pounds."

Felicity Fischer trumpeted in rage and tossed Cray into a rose bush. Loud squeals emitted from it.

Mr Snook ran over to pull him out. "Are you hurt?"

"I'm OK." Cray extracted himself. "Thanks."

Felicity Fischer lumbered over to me. "You. You do it. Turn me back this instant."

I stood my ground. "I will if you agree to shut your factory," I said. "And give all your money to the Institute of Science, and never cause any more damage to the environment."

"All of those things." Felicity Fischer nodded amiably. "I'll even join your dad's society, if you like."

I blinked in surprise. "You will?"

Felicity Fischer poked me hard in the chest. "Of course I won't," she hissed. "And if you don't reset me, I shall step on you and all your little friends – and then I'll nip back to the house and step on your father as well."

I stared at her. "You wouldn't," I said.

"I would." Felicity Fischer sniggered nastily. "Your poor mother. I'd have to tell her everything – and you'd get the blame for messing about with her invention."

"You're horrible," I said.

"I am, aren't I?" Felicity smirked at us.

I looked over at Penny and Chip, and Dr Cray and Mr Snook, and thought about Dad, and how upset Mum would be if we were all squashed flat.

I shrugged. "OK," I said. "I'll do it."

Felicity Fischer gave a satisfied smile. "I knew you would."

I stared up at her. "You're a bit high."

"Let me." Felicity Fischer grabbed the back of my shirt and swung me over her head.

I landed on her shaggy rump.

Oh my.

I took a moment.

I was sitting on a *mammoth*.

No one had sat on a mammoth for about ten thousand years.

How incredible was that!

I dug my hands into Felicity Fischer's woolly pelt and marvelled at it.

If only I could tell Mum about this.

I didn't have much time to feel special.

"What are you *doing*?" Felicity Fischer bellowed. "Hurry up."

"Sorry." I crawled along her back and reached for the cable dangling from her ear. I used it to very carefully pull Mum's machine towards me. The second it was close enough, I reached down and grabbed it.

I made sure nothing was broken, then attached the second cable to Felicity's other ear.

I didn't *want* to change her back.

If only there was another way.

I looked down at Penny to see if she had anything, but she just shrugged miserably.

Chip just gave me an evil stare.

No help from there, then.

It was at that *very* second Gertie chose to scramble out of my pocket.

She scampered over my leg and up on to Felicity Fischer's head.

Gertie! I stared at her in joy.

Felicity Fischer shifted impatiently beneath me. "Is there an issue?" she trumpeted.

"Almost done," I called down. "I'm just checking everything's working."

I pressed the button that opened the drawer and scooped out the mammoth DNA.

Then I picked up Gertie.

Lovely fluffy Gertie.

I watched her whiskers twitching for a moment, then tugged a tiny hair from under her chin.

She didn't seem to mind.

I put her safely back in my pocket, and then I put the

hair into the drawer and pushed it shut. "Ready?" I called.

"Do get on with it!" Felicity Fischer snapped.

I picked up Mum's machine and held it tight. I didn't press the reset button, though. I twisted the dial.

I listened as it ticked back round.

And then I shut my eyes and braced for impact.

There was a flash and a sizzle and a terrible smell of burning.

I hit the grass hard. That's because Felicity Fischer, as a mammoth, was big, and Felicity Fischer, as a hamster, wasn't.

"Percy!" Penny ran over and knelt down beside me. "What happened? Are you OK?"

"Just winded," I said, weakly. "Take the machine."

Mr Snook plucked it from my arms. "I have no idea what you did there, Percy, but very well done."

Cray was looking around with a puzzled expression.

I pulled Gertie out to check her over.

Penny's mouth dropped open. "Did you—?"

I nodded.

"You turned Felicity into a *hamster*?" Cray looked

delighted. He slapped me on the back. "Well done, Percy. *Very* well done." He scanned the ground. "Where is she, though? I can't see her."

I stood up and looked. I couldn't see her either.

I could *hear* something though. A ferocious yapping. It was coming from the direction of the sandpit.

I felt the colour drain from my face. I stared at Penny. "You don't think...?"

"I do," she said.

We turned and ran.

Felicity Fischer was lucky. We got there just in time. I rugby-tackled Chip as he made his final lunge.

"Got her!" Penny scooped Felicity Fischer up.

She didn't seem at all grateful to be rescued. She squeaked some very insulting things and bit Penny twice before Cray found a Happy Meal box to put her in.

"Won't she nibble her way out?" Penny asked.

"If she *did*," I said, "she might get eaten by a fox ... or an owl. So she probably won't."

There was a furious squeak from inside.

"I'll take her back to the house," Cray said. "I'll keep her in Gertie's cage for now."

"I'll come," I said. "I need to unstick Dad and Mrs Miggins from their chairs. And we need to re-extinct the broad-billed parrot."

"Excuse me." Penny raised her hand. "Before anyone goes *anywhere*, I'd like to turn Chip back, if you don't mind?"

"Of course!" Mr Snook ran over with the machine.

"I guess you'll have to tell Mum about all this?" I said, gloomily.

"I was thinking about that," Mr Snook said. "I could possibly *not* … if *you* don't mention that I thought she stole the gene blender for her own gain."

"Sounds fair," I said.

"Excellent," said Mr Snook.

By the time we got back to Felicity Fischer's mansion, Dad and Mrs Miggins had wiggled themselves free of the glue. Dad was VERY relieved to see us. "I thought I'd have to tell Mum you'd been squashed by a mammoth," he said. "Then she would have asked where the mammoth came from – and that would have opened a *whole* can of worms!" He looked anxious. "We're not going to say anything, are we?"

"It's probably best if we don't," I said. "I mean, there's no *need*, is there?"

"There certainly isn't," Dad agreed. He looked around. "Where's Felicity now?"

Penny pointed to the hamster cage. "She's having some time out," she said. "To think about her badness."

"That'll take a while." Dad sniffed.

I was pleased to see he'd found some clothes to borrow, even if the shoulders on the jacket were a bit pointy. He gave me a twirl. "What do you think?" he asked.

"Better than the poncho," I said. "Dad?"

"Yes?"

"Would you mind if I kept Gertie?" I held her up.

Dad narrowed his eyes. "She's not blended with anything is she? An alligator, or a vampire bat?"

I shook my head. "No."

He patted my shoulder. "That's fine then."

Cray was talking to Mrs Miggins. "Mr Snook's just reset the parrot," he said, "so you can have your chickens back."

Mrs Miggins glared at him. "I don't give refunds."

"I don't want one." Cray handed her the box.

"Oh, OK," Mrs Miggins said. "Thanks."

I went over. "Mrs Miggins," I said, "if you sold your chickens to Cray, why did the newspaper say they were stolen?"

"I have no *idea* where they got the story from," Mrs Miggins snapped. "It definitely wasn't from me." She looked around. "Do you think there are any more biscuits?"

TWENTY-EIGHT

Mum was cross at breakfast the next morning. "I don't know what work were thinking," she said. "I went all that way to do the DNA sample and the zoo was *full* of curly crested Chinese geese. They're not endangered in the slightest!"

"That's good." Dad scraped burnt bits off his toast. "For the Chinese geese, I mean." He looked up at Mum. "What time did you get in?"

"Just after midnight." Mum beamed at me and Penny. "Ella said she hadn't heard a peep out of either of you."

"We tried not to be any bother." Penny beamed back.

Dad reached for the jam. "Mr Snook dropped by yesterday."

Mum blinked. "Did he?"

Dad nodded. "He said he appreciated what you were trying to do, but our spare room wasn't suitable for the ... um..." He glanced at me.

I gazed out the window.

"... *thing* you had in there. He went up and got it and took it back to the lab."

"Oh?" Mum looked worried. "I'm not in trouble, am I?"

"Oh no," Dad reassured her. "He was pleased you'd shown such commitment to its safety."

"That's good." Mum looked relieved.

Dad went on. "He said he'd worked out who was trying to steal it."

"That's marvellous!" Mum was delighted. "Did he say who?"

Dad shook his head. "No. Just that they'd been moved from their position, and you didn't need to worry."

"That's a relief." Mum poured herself a cup of tea.

"How was your demonstration?"

"The glue was *extremely* effective," Dad said. "I think, this time, we really made a difference."

"Wonderful, wonderful," Mum clinked her mug against his. "I hope you didn't get cold?"

"It was a tad nippy," Dad admitted. "I'll wear something at the next one."

"Where is it?" I asked.

"The fruit and veg aisle at the Co-op." Dad looked excited. "We're going to highlight the carbon footprint of exotic produce. I'm going to paint myself red to symbolize the blood of creatures lost to climate change, and Mrs Miggins is going to dress as a banana."

"It sounds excellent," Penny said. "Can I come?"

"Of course!" Dad said. He turned to me. "What about you, Percy?"

"I wouldn't miss it," I said.

Mum almost choked on her tea.

"We all have to do our bit," I explained.

"I'm about to make some banners." Dad jumped up. "Do you want to help?"

"We will later," I said. "The prime minister's guinea pig is still missing. We're going to look for it. Come on, Penny."

Dad followed us into the hall, then checked Mum wasn't in earshot. "Mrs Miggins might have some information on the guinea pig," he muttered.

I stared at him. "What do you mean?"

"It wasn't stolen; it escaped. Mrs Miggins found it scampering down the street and … um … *saw an opportunity.*" Dad lowered his voice to a whisper. "She popped it in her shopping trolley and took it home."

I could scarcely believe my ears. "Mrs Miggins had it all along?"

Dad nodded. "By the time *I* found out, she'd already sent the ransom note. 'The guinea pig in exchange for reduced global emissions' it said."

I stared at him with my mouth open.

Dad went on. "And to deflect suspicion, she sold two of her chickens, then reported them stolen!"

"That's *genius!*" I said.

"*Illegal*, you mean," Dad huffed.

"I'd never have thought it of Mrs Miggins," Penny said. "Kidnap! She seems so respectable."

"It was for a good cause," I argued.

"That may be, Percy," Dad said, "but she could have brought my society into disrepute! I had to have words with her. Anyway, she's returning it this morning."

I'd been looking forward to solving the mystery of the pet thief, so after Dad's revelation, I felt a bit flat. Penny said that, instead, we should go and buy a little brush for Gertie, so her coat would be shiny for the show.

We took Chip along for the walk to the pet shop. Now Penny and I were getting along better, he was slightly more pleasant towards me. Not *super* friendly, but not primed to kill.

Cray and Mr Snook were in the small animal aisle.

They were holding hands.

"Aw, isn't that sweet." Penny gave them a wave.

"Good morning!" Cray bounded over.

"Hi," I said. "How's Felicity Fischer?"

"We're getting her some treats." Cray held up a packet of rodent choc drops. "She's developed loads of hamster traits. She's ever so good on her wheel! Goes for miles."

"We were going to change her back – but there was a hiccup with the machine," Mr Snook said.

Cray blushed. "I accidentally spilled some of your dad's glue into it. The whole thing seized up."

"It could take some time to fix." Mr Snook didn't sound too upset. "Years even. The parts are made in China, and you know what the post's like."

"In the meantime, I've put myself in charge of Felicity's assets," Cray said. "I am one of her closest relatives, after all."

"We've closed the factory," Mr Snook said.

"That's fantastic!" I said. "Dad will be over the moon."

"And as hamsters aren't allowed to tarmac parks or send billionaires into space – we're using the money to fund further investment into the rewilding programme." Cray looked mighty pleased with himself.

"Doesn't Felicity mind?" I asked.

"I didn't hear Felicity *say* she minded." Cray turned to Mr Snook. "Did you, Amos?"

Mr Snook shook his head. "No. Unless we forgot to ask."

"I distinctly think I remember not forgetting to ask." Cray said.

"So that's that, then," Mr Snook said happily.

"Your Dad will have to find something else to protest about," Penny said to me.

I eyed the traffic streaming past outside. "Don't worry," I said. "I'm sure there's plenty."

"Isn't it nice Cray's found a friend," Penny said on the way home. "Felicity Fischer was so mean to him." She handed me something. "I got you this. They were for sale in the pet shop."

It was a poster. I unrolled it, then blinked. "Hetta Bunberg?" I said.

"I thought you could put it in your room," Penny said.

"Maybe not my actual *room*," I said, "but I'll find somewhere for it. Thanks."

Penny pointed up the road. "Look," she said. "There's Mrs Miggins. Shall we say hello?"

We crossed over to join her.

"Have you been to take the guinea pig back?" Penny asked.

Mrs Miggins gave an excellent impression of not knowing what we were talking about.

"Dad told us," I said.

Mrs Miggins scowled. "I can't believe he didn't approve," she said. "It was a really good idea."

"It was certainly creative," Penny said, kindly.

"We're coming to your exotic fruit protest," I said. "The one at the Co-op. Have you got your costume yet?"

Mrs Miggins brightened. "It arrived earlier. Would you like to see it?"

"Please," I said.

We sat in Mrs Miggins's kitchen while she went to get

changed. There were some eggs on the side in a bowl. Three were normal looking chicken eggs, but one was much smaller and a funny shade of blue.

After we'd admired Mrs Miggins dressed as a banana, I asked her about the egg.

"One of the hens laid it this morning," she said. "I expect she was out of sorts after the kerfuffle at Felicity Fischer's. Can't be much fun being a parrot."

I picked the egg up for a closer look. It was still warm, and very pretty. "Could I keep it?" I asked.

Mrs Miggins gave it some thought. "Two quid and it's yours," she said.

I only had a pound left after buying Gertie's brush, so I borrowed another from Penny, as well as 50p for an empty margarine tub to take it home in.

"That's a bit steep for an egg," Penny muttered as we left.

"I know," I said. "But it'll be worth it to *see*."

"See *what*?" she asked.

A few months later, Gertie took first prize in the

hamster category at the Great Potton Pet Show. Cray and Mr Snook were there to cheer her on.

Chip was disqualified from the elderly dachshund class for taking a disliking to the judge. Penny was furious. "He was being friendly," she said.

Best in show was awarded to my broad-billed parrot. The judges said they'd never seen anything like her.

I didn't tell them why.

I just basked in the glory.

Author's note

Dear Reader,

When I was small, I didn't have a phone, or an Xbox – but I did have a badge that read: "LOOK AFTER YOUR EARTH, YOU CAN'T GET OFF". My family were activists, and most weekends we'd pack up our sandwiches and our hand-painted placards and head off to a demo. We marched to save the whale and we marched against pesticides and we marched against the effects of pollution on the environment. We knew biodiversity was in decline, but what we didn't know was that a mass extinction of our own making was just around the corner.

In the forty years since I made my first placard, the number of wild animals living on earth has fallen by half. Poachers killed the last western black rhino, climate change saw off the golden toad, and the Pinta giant tortoise lost its habitat to domestic goats. The extinction rate is now a thousand times higher than before humans dominated the planet. Through activities that accelerate climate change, the obliteration of rainforests and the polluting of oceans, humans are destroying the ecosystems all species need to survive.

The creatures Percy's mum is trying to save roamed a rich and diverse landscape that no longer exists. If agricultural activities continue unchecked, a further one million species will face extinction within decades.

It's not too late to reverse things. Rewilding lets nature take care of itself, enabling natural processes to restore damaged ecosystems. Once habitats are re-established, plant and animal species that have been driven out can be returned. A century from now, our world could be wild again.

It'll take a lot of people working together to make this change happen. If you'd like to, there are ways you can help:

You could stand up against deforestation by avoiding foods that contain unsustainable palm oil.

Fight plastic pollution by using reusable water bottles, bringing reusable bags with you to the shops, and always taking your rubbish home.

Try cycling, walking, or using public transport rather than the car.

Rewild an area in your garden or school playground. Sprinkle some soil around and let daisies and dandelions grow. Wildflowers provide food for bees, who are important for pollinating food crops. You could encourage hedgehogs to visit by leaving leaves and twigs for them to nest in. You could build an insect hotel, make a log pile, or even dig a pond.

Join Friends of the Earth (www.friendsoftheearth.uk), or Extinction Rebellion (www.extinctionrebellion.uk).

Go to a demo and shout as loud as you can.

And the most important thing? Share your

knowledge with others. Help them to help the environment too.

Together, we'll get there.

We have to.

Acknowle
 ents

A mammoth thank you to...

Linas Alsenas, for his most excellent

editing. tful

Fay Austin, for her fabulous illustrations.

Liam Drane, who made this book so smar

shiny.

The rest of the wondrous Scholastic team, including Emily Hibbs for the extremely thorough copyedit, Catherine Liney for the proofread and Sarah Dutton for pulling it all together.

The amazing Kate Shaw, agent of the century.

Ruth Griffiths, the best kind of writerly friend.

The lovely Julie Pike, for her guidance on eco matters.

The usual crowd. I couldn't do this without you.

And Isobel, Eva, Hattie and Daisy, who fill my life with joy and unwashed mugs.

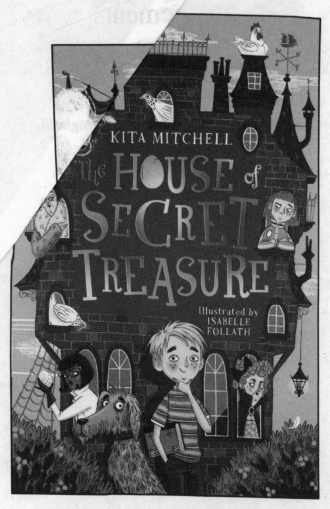

KITA MITCHELL

The HOUSE of SECRET TREASURE

Illustrated by
ISABELLE FOLLATH